KU-369-539

Murder
Among
Children

Tucker Coe

NO EXIT PRESS

1990

No Exit Press
18 Coleswood Rd
Harpenden, Herts, AL5 1EQ

Copyright © Donald Westlake 1967

First U.K. Publication 1968

All rights reserved. No part of this book may be
reproduced, stored in a retrieval system, or transmitted,
in any form, or by any means, electronic, mechanical,
photocopying, recording or otherwise, without the
written permission of the publishers.

British Library Cataloguing in Publication Data
– record available

ISBN 0 948353 69 4

9 8 7 6 5 4 3 2 1

Miss S / Mrs.

1 ———————————

THREE happy children came walking down the street from my right. They were chattering together in Italian, and waving their arms, and laughing at one another. As they neared me, one of them looked up and caught my eye and said something brisk and happy to me. I had no idea what he was saying, but the tone was cheerful and the smiles on all three faces seemed guileless, so I smiled back and said, "Hello, yourselves." Then they passed me, the traffic light changed, and I crossed the street and walked deeper into the West Village, that part of lower Manhattan Island situated between Greenwich Village and the Hudson River.

I was now on Charles Street, west of Hudson; the address I wanted proved to be a block and a half farther on. Amid trucking-company sheds and storage warehouses, four red-brick tenements were squared off together like pieces left over from a giant antique Monopoly board, and it was the last of these I wanted. It differed from the others both in its lack of a high front stoop and in the existence of a shop on the ground floor. The plate-glass windows flanking the shop entrance had been painted black, with white stick figures painted on to represent couples sitting at round tables, one couple and one table to each window. Above the doorway a wooden sign was suspended from a metal rod; against a black background it said, in wavery white letters:

THING EAST

I stood a moment outside, and looked around. This was a Sunday in late August, hot with the usual August humidity, the late-morning sun beating down on a silent and deserted street. Except for these tenements there were no residences on this block, and none of the firms along here would be open today. Few people were out now anywhere in Manhattan; those who weren't away on vacation were at the beaches or lying on beds in air-conditioned rooms. The subway I'd taken in from Queens had been almost as empty as this street.

When at last I pushed open the door and went inside Thing East, I thought at first that it too was deserted, empty except for me. It was a very dim room, made darker by contrast with the brightness outside. I stood just within the door, squinting, and tried to make out the interior.

The room was long and rather narrow. Both side walls were bare brick, liberally hung with large black and white photographs and larger abstract paintings. The ceiling was of old-fashioned tin, painted a dull black, and from it were suspended a number of amber globes containing low-wattage bulbs, as though someone had calculated to within a fraction of a lumen the minimum amount of light required to read a menu by. Three lines of small square wooden tables stretched down the length of the room, flanked by chairs of widely varying types, ranging from delicate filigree ironwork to the bluntest of wooden kitchen chairs. Centered on each table was a large full glass sugar dispenser, and next to each sugar dispenser were squat glass salt and pepper shakers. At the far end of the room was a waist-high counter, past which could be seen a brightly lit and apparently empty kitchen.

I stepped forward, put one hand on the back of a chair, and called, "Hello? Anyone here?"

I was answered by sudden movement at the far end of the room.

From the last table in the right-hand row a man arose and came toward me, saying, "You want something, mister?"

My first impression of him was of a rough-hewn maleness. His hair was thick and brown, his face was dominated by a full shaggy brown mustache, and he was wearing black slacks and a maroon turtleneck sweater. A dirty white towel was tucked crosswise into the top of his trousers, apron-fashion, covering him from waist to thigh. His nose, above the Cossack mustache, was wide and flaring. He was tall, and seemed husky within the sweater.

But as he approached, the image began to crack and shatter, as in an accelerated process of decay, and I saw that he was much younger than I had at first supposed, no more than twenty or twenty-one, and his eyes belied the appearance of masculinity, being young and sullen and uncertain. He worked, like an actor on stage, only at a distance, but of course he was still young and he might yet grow into the part.

I said, "I'm looking for Robin Kennely."

His expression grew guarded, and he said, "What do you want with her?"

I understood the expression, having seen it hundreds of times over the years. It meant that he had smelled the smell of cop on me and was prepared to protect himself and everyone he knew from me until the last bitter silence. When the New York Police Department had taken my badge away they had been unable to strip me also of that telltale scent; it entered every situation with me, adding irony to the intolerability of my life.

I couldn't deny being a cop, however, since I hadn't in so many words been accused of being one. But I could give this young man a different *persona* for me, so I said, "I'm a relative of hers."

He looked at me in disbelief. "The cousin?"

"Second cousin, yes."

"I thought—" He gestured vaguely, and looked over my shoulder as though someone behind me would resolve his confusion.

"Not all cousins," I explained, "are the same age. Robin Kennely is my mother's sister's granddaughter. Is she here?"

"Sure. Upstairs. Up in Terry's place."

"How do I get there?"

"Come on through the back," he said, and turned away, and said over his shoulder as he walked, "I thought you'd be a young guy. I don't know why, I just got the idea."

There was nothing to say to that. We walked in single file down the long room and through a doorway on the right side into the kitchen, a wide shallow room all in white and aluminum, illuminated by garish fluorescent lights.

"The stairs are through that door," the young man said, and as he pointed the door opened and Robin Kennely came through, smeared with great streaks of not-dry blood. The knife in her hand was carmine with it.

"There's a certain thing," she said, enunciating clearly in a high thin cold voice, and collapsed on the floor.

2 ———————————

I HAD first met Robin Kennely just the day before, when she had come to see me at my house in Queens. I was in back, working on my wall, when Kate came out to say, "There's a girl here to see you."

That made no sense. Because of past history I felt a flickering instant of frightened guilt, but there was nothing in the now to feel guilty about, so it went away. I rested on my shovel and said, "Who is she?"

I was standing in the hole I was digging, and Kate stood over me. If you are going to build a wall, and if it is to be a good wall, long-lasting, solid, dependable, it is necessary first to dig. The wall must start in the ground, down below the frost line. Working slowly, carefully, working perhaps no more than a day or two a week, I had in the last several months dug about half of the necessary trench, putting down one level layer of concrete block in my wake, to guard against erosion of the sides. I was in no particular hurry to finish my wall; its construction was its own purpose.

What Kate understands of my wall, or of me, I do not know. She is my wife, and she has chosen to stay with me, and I am grateful without curiosity. I fear sometimes that like a fragile flower, the life I have constructed for myself will crumble if I ever submit it to investigation, so I walk softly, I work slowly on my wall, I do not feel curiosity.

Kate said, "She says she's a cousin of yours. Robin Kennely."

"A cousin? I never heard of her."

"She says her mother is your cousin Rita Gibson."

That name I knew. I have never been much for maintaining broad family ties, but I did remember from my childhood a thin angular black-haired girl named Cousin Rita Gibson. Aunt Agnes Gibson's daughter.

I said, "All right. Tell her I'll be there in a few minutes. I have to clean up."

"All right."

Kate preceded me. I carried my shovel and level to the back porch and left them there, took off my work gloves, left them outside also, and went on into the house.

Kate was already in the living room with the girl. I heard them talking. It was necessary for me to go past the living-room door to get to the stairs, which I did without looking in at them. I went up, washed, changed out of my work clothes, and came back down to find they had both transferred to the kitchen, where the girl was sitting at my usual place at the table while Kate was in the process of making coffee.

The irrational is never very far away. I found myself taking an immediate dislike to this girl, partly because of the instant of guilt she had made me feel when Kate had first announced her presence, partly because she was sitting in my chair, and partly because she was very young and very beautiful.

I would guess her age at eighteen. She was slender, fine-boned, with long neck and delicate wrists. Her hair was a smooth and glossy black, worn straight and very long, in the manner of girl folk singers on television. Her face was fine-featured and bare of make-up and dominated by large level intelligent brown eyes. She was wearing a conservative pale green suit and a white blouse with a ruffle at the throat, an outfit designed as office wear for a secretary of age thirty. That she had made such a determined child's effort to dress up for this meeting gave some indication of its importance to her.

Strangling my stupid enmity, I came on into the kitchen and said, "How do you do?"

She sprang to her feet, lithe and new as a colt. "How do you do?" She gave me a quick trusting embarrassed smile and said, "I don't know what to call you. Cousin Mitchell? Mr. Tobin?"

"I think just Mitch. And you're Robin?"

"Yes. Robin Kennely. My mother is—"

"Yes, I understood that." Then I saw by her face that I'd been rude, and I tried to produce a friendly smile as I said, "Sit down, sit down. You don't have to be ceremonious with a cousin."

Kate brought over cups and plates then, breaking the awkward moment, and I sat across the table from the girl and tried to think of some kind of small talk. But there hadn't been any small talk in me for a long while, not since my life had ended, and there wasn't any now.

Bless Kate. While she moved here and there around the kitchen, preparing coffee, getting cookies, she kept a conversation alive with the girl, asking her questions about her mother and her grandmother and all my other relatives, some of whom Kate herself knew slightly and many of whom she had never met.

When at last we were all three sitting around the table, Kate allowed the conversation to lapse, and after a minute the girl looked at me and said, "Well, I guess I ought to get to it."

"Take your time," I said. "Have another cookie."

She reflexively reached out to the plate for another, but then just held it in her hand as she spoke. "You see," she said, looking very young and very earnest, "I was the only one who even knew a policeman at all."

"I'm not a policeman," I said quickly, but then I saw Kate stiffen and I realized I'd spoken too loudly and harshly, so I said, "But I still know some. What do you need a policeman for?"

"It's hard to explain," she said, "without it being all a jumble. My boy friend is—I have a boy friend, Terry Wilford, he's opening a coffee house. Down in the Village, you know? Terry and three other boys, they put their money in together. We've got—they've got a store they rented. It was very lucky, it isn't expensive at all, and there's a contingency lease, if the shop fails in three months they don't have to keep the lease any more."

She had grown too involved in her explanation to be able to talk without her hands, so she'd put the unwanted cookie back on the plate and was now leaning over the coffee cup, elbows on the table, hands waving expressively, eyes urgent and intent on me as she talked. I could see her just this way at a table in her boy friend's coffee house; in our slow and heavy household she was out of place, improbable and slightly fabulous.

I said, "It sounds as though you already have a lawyer. I don't know the problem yet, but have you talked it over with him?"

"George isn't really a lawyer," she said, and smiled abruptly, a startlingly sunny sight. "It's actually sort of funny," she said. "George's older brother works for the Post Office and goes nights to NYU. He's been studying to be a lawyer for nine years, and George says he'll never make it. But whenever we want to know anything legal, George goes and asks his brother. But that won't do us any good now."

"Why not?"

"Well . . . We just opened last Monday. And Wednesday a man came around, a policeman. He wouldn't say what he wanted, he just kept asking questions and looking around and being very—in-sinuating. As though we were doing something wrong and he was onto us. And he kept talking about how it would be too bad if somebody had to close us down."

"Was he in uniform?"

"No. But George wanted to see his identification, and he really was a policeman. A detective."

"All right. What did he finally do?"

"Wednesday, he just left after a while. But then he came back Thursday night, and he kept saying about how everybody has to fit into a neighborhood, you can't have people who don't fit in, and then last night he was there again and went around asking all the customers for identification. And always insinuating, insinuating. Like because Terry lives upstairs, and Thursday when he came I was upstairs and when I came down he wanted to know if girls upstairs was going to be a feature of the place."

I could feel Kate looking at me. The cop on the take had always been a pet peeve of ours when I was on the force, and this story of Robin Kennely's had all the earmarks. I said, "So then what happened?"

She made a very young shrugging motion, dipping her head, and said, "Well, George says what he wants is money. A pay-off. That's what his brother says, the almost lawyer. And we know about things like that, I mean there were all kinds of funny fees to the Housing Department and this and that, and there was a man came around from the Fire Department and kept talking about how we had to have more entrances and more fire extinguishers, and George's brother talked to him and gave him fifty dollars. But this policeman is so *weird*. Everybody's afraid to offer him money, because what if that isn't it? Then we're really in trouble."

"You haven't offered him a bribe."

She shook her head. "We're not cynics, Mr. Tobin," she said, forgetting that she was supposed to call me Mitch. "But we know that if you're going to do something you have to do like everybody else does. We knew we'd have to pay some people extra money. But this policeman acts so strange, we aren't really sure. We don't know if we should pay him, or how much, or anything. And George's brother doesn't want to take the chance of offering him money because what if he wasn't there for a bribe? Then George's brother would be in trouble. Well, we'd all be in trouble."

"What other reason do you think he might have, if he doesn't want money?"

She seemed hesitant, and when she answered this time she looked more frequently at Kate than at me. "Some people," she said, "some policemen and people like that, they think young people in the Village— Well, they're down on young people. They think we're all beatniks and immoral and everything. You'll see policemen give somebody a bad time just because he has a beard, or a girl just because she's in the Village. So that's what it might be, he just wants to make a little trouble because he doesn't like us. And if that's it, we'd make an awful mistake if we tried to give him money. It would just make everything a lot worse."

I said, "Is that what your friend Terry thinks?"

A sudden blush colored her cheeks, and she said, "Terry thinks he wants a girl."

"You?"

"Maybe me. Or maybe just a girl. Terry says he's one of those— one of those people who thinks everybody around coffee houses still believes in free love."

"So Terry thinks he wants a non-money bribe, is that it?"

She nodded.

I said, "And you want to ask me what I think, is that it?"

"In a way," she said. "But—" She hesitated, looked at Kate, looked helplessly back at me, and made her dipping-shrugging movement again.

Kate spoke up for the first time, saying, "Mitch, does it sound like a pay-off?"

"Almost," I said. "It could be something else, I don't know. But that's most likely."

Kate said to the girl, "And you want Mitch to talk to him, is that it?"

I looked at the two of them, startled. I'd had no idea. I'd been thinking the girl had simply come to me for advice, for my opinion about what this cop wanted, and I'd been trying to make up my mind what I should tell her. It did sound very much like a guy on the make, wanting a little white envelope now and again to encourage him not to make trouble, but it wasn't absolutely definite as yet, and I didn't want to give these youngsters advice that would get them in worse trouble. So I'd been thinking about it, trying to find other questions to ask that might help me make up my mind, and it had never occurred to me that this new-found relative of mine might actually want me to get up and go out and *do* something.

But that was what she wanted. Kate had guessed it, and Kate was right, as she very often is about the unexpressed needs of others. Robin Kennely leaped gratefully at Kate's suggestion, saying, "Oh, yes! None of us can do it, we really can't." And then turned to me, pleading, saying, "Could you possibly?"

"Well," I said. I felt trapped. I didn't want to leave this house, for Robin Kennely or anybody else. I'd left it a few months ago, driven by economic need, doing a piece of work for enough money to make it possible for me to stay in here for maybe a year or more, but that was the only time I'd gone out and it had not made me want to repeat the experience in a hurry.

I could feel Kate looking at me, but I refused to meet her eyes. She wanted me to go with the girl, I knew that, and only partly because Kate had taken an immediate liking to her. The rest of it was that she believed it would be better for me to be in motion than to remain stagnant. She was wrong about this, but I couldn't blame her for thinking it.

The girl said, "Please, Mr. Tobin. If you would, if you only would. We've put everything we've got into this, and if it fails we're in terrible trouble. And if this man keeps coming around, nobody will come, we'll lose everything. Please."

I said, "What's this policeman's name?"

"Edward Donlon," she said. "Detective Second Grade."

"About how old?"

She shrugged; too old. "I don't know," she said. "I suppose about fifty."

Which meant anything over forty. Young people have a tendency to overestimate the age of their elders. I said, "What does he look like?"

Before she could answer, Kate said, "Mitch, go see him for yourself. It's the only way."

"Not necessarily," I said. "It still might be something else."

"All the more reason," she said.

The girl said, "He told us he'd be back Sunday. Tomorrow. Sunday afternoon, he said."

"You can see him then," Kate told me.

"I could phone one or two people," I said. "I still know people on the force." To the girl I said, "What precinct are you in?"

Kate said, "Mitch, you can't mean that. Do you want to make things worse?"

Robin Kennely was looking back and forth at the two of us, her expression getting more and more stricken, and now, falteringly, she said, "If you don't want to—"

But I could see it was impossible. I'd have to give over a day to it. The idea of talking to somebody on the force, somebody who maybe knew my name, knew what I'd done, made my neck muscles tight with tension, even though the likelihood was slim. There were thousands of men on the force, and less than two hundred of them were likely to make any connection with the name Mitchell Tobin.

That thought didn't help me much. Still, I knew there was nothing else open to me. I would have to take the subway into Manhattan tomorrow, and talk to this heavy-handed cop, and see what I could do to help these children with their coffee house. There wasn't even any point telling Robin Kennely the coffee house was doomed anyway, no matter what I did or did not succeed in doing. These frail businesses start up all the time, particularly on the fringes of Greenwich Village. They are begun by wide-eyed youngsters with fuzzy goals and fuzzier business comprehension, they stagger along for a few months, and then they collapse, usually in small-claims court, sometimes in a flurry of bad checks. I'd picked up my share of debt-ridden child entrepreneurs while I was on the force, and I'd gotten so I could tell at a glance the businesses that were not going to make it through their first fiscal year.

But I said none of this to Robin Kennely. What I said was, "I'll come. What time tomorrow, did he say?"

3 ————————————————————

AFTERNOON. And now it was Sunday afternoon, and I had arrived at Thing East, and Robin Kennely, blood-smeared and still clutching the butcher knife, lay unconscious at my feet.

I said to the mustached boy, "Go lock the front door. Where's your phone?"

There wasn't any answer. I looked at him, and he was staring at the girl on the floor, his face blank-white and his mouth slack. I took his arm, shook it. "Snap out of it. Go lock the front door. Tell me where the phone is."

He started, and blinked, and shook his head, as though awakened suddenly from a deep sleep. He turned wide eyes on me. "Phone," he said. "On the wall there." And pointed at the opposite end of the kitchen.

"Good. Go lock the door."

"Yes. Yes, sir."

He went away, and I headed for the phone. I dialed the police emergency number, gave my name and location, and said, "Send a squad car, there's been trouble here. Looks like a knifing. We'll need an ambulance, too."

I hung up, and went out front, and found the young man standing by the front door like a mannequin no longer needed in the window. I said, "Did you lock it?"

He looked at me as though he were afraid of me. "Yes," he said, and reached out to rattle the knob.

I said, "Are there any other stairs? Any other way up?"

He shook his head.

"There's at least one," I told him. "The fire escape. Where's that? In back?"

"Yes. In back."

"Any other way? *Think, boy.*"

He blinked again. "No other way," he said. "Just the stairs, those stairs. And the fire escape."

"All right. Stand here. I've phoned for a squad car and ambulance. When they get here, let them in. Don't let anybody else in. You got that?"

He nodded.

"Good. What's your name?"

"George," he said. "George Padbury."

"You the one with the almost-lawyer brother?"

"Yes," he said, surprised. "Ralph. My brother Ralph."

"Who's upstairs now?"

"Upstairs?"

"That you know of."

"Well— Just Terry."

"Terry Wilford?"

He nodded again. "He lives up there."

"He's one of the tenants."

"He's the only tenant," Padbury said. "It's all empty up there, all the rest of it."

"All right. Stay here."

"I will."

I hurried back down the long room, through the entranceway into the white kitchen, and found Robin Kennely still out. She was breathing, fitfully, and beneath the smears of blood her face was pale.

I went past her, found a door between a sink and a stove, opened it, and rediscovered sunlight.

And heat. The difference between this cool grotto-like world and the reality outside was astonishing. Humid heat flooded inward, engulfing me, as I opened the door, and I felt the perspiration springing to the surface on my forehead and arms.

I stepped through the doorway into a square gray-white concrete box, open at the top. High walls extended on all four sides, featureless to my left and right, windowed in front of me and above my head. A fire escape made a harsh black pattern against the rear wall of the building I had just stepped out of, but no similar pattern showed on the wall opposite. One look was enough to see that there was no way into that building over there from here; the nearest windows were not only ten feet or more from the ground, but were also barred.

No one had left since Robin Kennely's melodramatic appearance at my feet. If the only two ways out were down the stairs that Robin had used or down the fire escape into this cul-de-sac, then whoever had been up there five minutes ago was still there.

I went back into the kitchen, shutting the door behind me, and saw Robin just beginning to sit up. Her movements were uncoordinated, slow, hesitant. I went over, squatted down beside her, and without touching her I said, "Can you tell me what happened?"

She looked at me with unfocused eyes. "Mr. Tobin?"

"What happened upstairs?"

She frowned in confused concentration. "Upstairs?"

"You don't remember?"

She moved a hand toward her face, then stopped and looked at it, at the streaks and smears of blood all over it. In the same tiny high voice she had used just before fainting she said, "What happened? What's happened to me?"

"I don't know," I said. "Don't try to stand, just stay where you are. I've called for the police."

She looked at me, bewildered. "Am I hurt?"

"I don't think so," I said. "I don't think that's your blood."

She looked at herself, and then saw the knife lying beside her on the floor. I tensed, but she didn't reach for it. She looked at it as though it were something she couldn't understand the meaning or purpose of, and then said, "But—" And that was all.

"The police will be here soon," I said. "We'll just wait for them." She didn't seem to hear me. She kept staring at the knife.

4

I DIDN'T know either of the uniformed men who initially answered the squeal. George Padbury let them in at the front, and they came down to where I was waiting in the kitchen doorway. I stayed there because I didn't want Robin Kennely—or the door to the stairs—out of my sight.

I identified myself—without any reference to my former connection with the force—described what had happened and what I'd done, and they took over. One of them double-checked the impossibility of using the fire escape for departure, and then they both went upstairs.

George Padbury had come back to the kitchen, and as soon as the patrolmen had gone out of sight he whispered to me, "What are they going to do?"

"Find something unpleasant, I think." I turned to Robin, still sitting on the floor, still dazed. "What are they going to find, Robin?"

She looked at me, but didn't say anything, and the three of us went on waiting. I didn't ask her the question any more because she clearly was incapable, at least right now, of answering it.

The patrolmen were upstairs perhaps three minutes, and came down together. They were both young, and right now they were both pale. One of them headed for the front while the other said to me, "You haven't been up there?"

"No."

There was noise from the front. I looked that way, and saw two men in white coming in as the patrolman was going out.

The other one, the one who had stayed to ask me if I'd been upstairs, had turned now to Robin, saying, "You want to talk about it?"

When she didn't answer him, I said, "Maybe we better let the medical men look at her."

He glanced at me, then past me, and took a step back. "In here," he said. "Take a look at her, number one. Then we got something upstairs."

The two ambulance men came into the kitchen, and now we were all crowded around the girl sitting on the floor. George Padbury had moved back against the wall and was looking at everybody as though afraid someone was about to pull a very dirty practical joke on him. The patrolman had that slightly uncomfortable expression of someone who has nothing to do but stand around and wait for somebody else to take over the job. The two ambulance men, both young, both with blue-gray jaws, looked efficient and phlegmatic. I felt uneasy and full of premonitions, being sucked into something more complicated and messy than I'd anticipated.

One of the ambulance men squatted down in front of Robin and said, "Wounded? What happened?"

I said, "She doesn't seem to be hurt, just in shock. That's somebody else's blood on her."

He looked up at me. "Detective squad?"

"No. Just a private citizen. I happened to be here."

He and the patrolman exchanged glances, and then he went back to concentrating on Robin. He got her to tell him her name, and to look at him, and to reel off parrot-like her address. But when the patrolman leaned down and asked her what had happened upstairs an aluminum gate clanged shut behind her eyes and there was nothing from her but silence.

The ambulance man said, "We better take her along with us."

"No," said the patrolman. "We'll wait till the boys from the squad show up."

The ambulance man shrugged and got to his feet. "You say you got more upstairs?"

"Right." The patrolman looked at me. "Why don't you sit down over there for a while?"

"All right."

George Padbury came over with me and we both sat down at the table where he'd been on my arrival. The two ambulance men went on upstairs. Robin Kennely continued to sit on the floor, and the patrolman stood near her, where he could watch the two of us at the table. The other patrolman was still out in the car, reporting.

I said to Padbury, "How long you been here?"

"You mean today?"

"Naturally."

"Oh. I thought you might mean how long've we been open. I've been here since maybe twelve-thirty."

I looked at my watch, which read five minutes to two. I said, "When was the last time you saw Robin? Before this time, I mean."

"When we came here."

"Today, at twelve-thirty?"

"Sure."

"The two of you came here together."

"The three of us," he said. "Robin and Terry and me. They picked me up at my place over in the East Village and drove me."

"You all came here together. Who was here?"

"Nobody. We don't open on Sunday till three."

"The place was locked? And empty?"

"Sure. Nobody lives here but Terry."

Slowly I got a complete story from him. He didn't seem particularly hostile or uncooperative, but he never answered any more than the immediate question I had asked, which made it all take longer than it should have.

What I finally got was mostly bad news. Until a recent warehouse construction on the block behind this one, the rear of this building had not been a cul-de-sac. But once that fourth side had been closed off, the fire escape on the rear of the building was no longer of any use, which meant the upper floors could not legally be occupied. Because of a door in the right side wall leading out to an alley, making two exits, this ground floor could still be used.

The building had been owned for the last several years by some small religious organization, which had used the upper floors as mission dormitories and the lower floor as a meeting room or chapel. They had converted the place to their own purposes, removing the outside steps from the front of the building, leaving only the inside staircase—and the fire escape, of course—as access to the upper floors.

When the Fire Department had informed this group that they could no longer use the building unless a fire escape was put on the front, they chose instead to move to new quarters. They hadn't yet decided what they were going to do with the old building, and had agreed to rent the ground floor to these young people for a coffee house, with the provision that either side could end the arrangement after three months.

There was also a provision that no use would be made of the upper floors except for storage of materials, but Terry Wilford had been violating that from the outset. He'd moved a few pieces of furniture to a second-floor room, and had lived there for a month now, ever since work had started on converting the first floor to a coffee house.

As to George Padbury, he lived on the Lower East Side, more fashionably known these days as the East Village. Terry Wilford and Robin had picked him up at his apartment today a little past noon and had driven him over here in Terry's car, a Volkswagen. The building was locked when they arrived, and gave no sign of any forcible entry. The three young people had entered, Padbury had gone to work in the kitchen, and the other two had gone upstairs. No one had entered or left since then, until my arrival an hour later.

When I said, "Did Robin and Terry fight a lot?" Padbury looked startled, glanced at Robin across the way, looked swiftly back at me, and said, "You don't think *she* did anything, do you?"

I said, "Only two people went upstairs. One of them is down here covered with blood. I heard one of the patrolmen say there was a body upstairs. It has to be Terry, and Robin has to have done it."

He shook his head stubbornly. "No, sir."

"If they don't find any third party up there," I said, "then she's it."

He kept shaking his head.

5

THE NEXT hour moved slowly, with me on the sidelines watching the well-remembered procedure. The precinct detectives arrived next, two of them, neither known to me. They got the story from one of the patrolmen, they looked around, they called in. Technical men began trooping in, carrying black cases, coming down the long aisle and into the kitchen and upstairs. The ambulance men took Robin Kennely away with them; she didn't look at me as she went by.

Two boys from Homicide South made a courtesy call and decided to stick around awhile. More precinct plainclothesmen arrived. The building was filling up with members of the force, and I knew it was only a matter of time till one of them was somebody I knew. More importantly, he would be somebody who knew me. Knew about me.

Padbury nudged my arm at one point, and whispered, "That's him. Coming out from the stairs."

I looked that way and saw a tall and heavy-set man of about forty, wearing a rumpled brown suit. He was very heavy in the jaw, making his eyes and forehead look smaller than they really were. If it hadn't been for that overstrong jaw, he would have been a handsome man, with a strong face and thick black hair.

I said, "That's Donlon?"

"Yeah, the cop that was coming around. That's him."

Donlon walked past us without a glance, heading for the front door, where he said something to the patrolman on guard there and then turned around and came back. He moved like a man who keeps himself in shape, probably at a gym. This time he paused as he went by us, his eyes cataloguing Padbury as someone he knew and then hesitating at me. He stopped, scanned me, seemed about to say something, and then went on. I watched him go through the door to the stairs.

Padbury said, "He gives me the creeps, man."

There was no reason for it. He looked like a man, that's all. If there was an aura of toughness, of implied menace, about him, that was merely the façade a lot of the boys on the force put up as a defense against cop-baiters, of which the world is full. Having seen him, I no longer had any question about his motives in hanging around this place all week. He was out for a touch and nothing more, it showed all over him.

A minute later the people from the morgue arrived. They went by me carrying two baskets, which didn't make any sense.

Padbury said, "What are those things for?"

"To carry bodies in," I said. "Why would there be two of them?"

He looked at me, wide-eyed. "What are you asking me for?"

"You said there was nobody else upstairs."

"That's right," he said.

"If there's only one body up there," I said, "why do they need two baskets?"

"*I* don't know. Maybe Terry got cut in half or something."

I shook my head. "Two baskets means two bodies," I said. "Who's the other one?"

"I swear to God," he said. "I swear to God I don't know. I left here last night about two in the morning, I come back today at twelve-thirty. If somebody went up there, I don't know about it."

"You haven't been up there yourself today."

"No, sir."

"Did Terry have any other girl friends?"

"No, sir. Just Robin. And she didn't have anybody else either."

The morgue attendants came through again, two men to a basket. They were both obviously heavy now. The attendants' faces were impassive.

I watched them leave, and saw another plainclothesman come in. He came down the aisle, started by me, stopped, looked at me, frowned, said, "Mitch?"

I looked up at him, and he had a face I knew. We'd been assigned to the same precinct a dozen years ago. I remembered his first name was Gregg, but couldn't recall the last name. I said, "Hello, Gregg."

He said, "You in on—?" And then he stopped, looked very puzzled, and glanced around as though to find someone to explain things to him. He'd obviously just remembered about me.

I said, "I'm a private citizen. I just happened to be here."

"Well," he said, and looked very uncomfortable. "Long time no see," he said.

"You're looking good," I said, for something to say.

"You, too. Well, I gotta get to work." He grinned painfully and said, "That's what they pay me for."

"Right."

He walked away, and a minute later I saw him talking to two of the other plainclothesmen. They both glanced my way, and then leaned their heads close to hear what Gregg had to say.

I knew what he was telling them. That I had been a cop, a plainclothesman working out of a precinct uptown, until the day my partner was shot and killed making an arrest that hadn't turned out to be as easy as it should have been. And he was killed because I wasn't there to back him up. And I wasn't there to back him up because at the moment he was dying I was in bed with a woman not my wife.

I closed my eyes, and waited inside there for whatever would happen next. If only I'd stayed home. I hadn't wanted to come out today.

George Padbury said, "You okay?" so I couldn't even close down that much.

I opened my eyes. "I'm okay," I said, and saw two of them coming over to talk with me.

6

IT WASN'T as painful as it might have been. Neither of them made any reference at all to my past history, though their knowledge of it shone in their eyes, slatelike.

They took me to another table, away from Padbury, and I told them my story. They wanted to ask into Robin's background, and it took me a while to make them understand that I really didn't know the girl. It wasn't that they disbelieved me, it was just hard to comprehend the fact that we were cousins who had never met before yesterday.

The whole interrogation took no more than ten minutes, and then they asked me to stick around a little while. One of them said, "You don't have any appointments anywhere, do you?"

"No," I said.

"We'll get back to you," he said, and they both got up and went away.

I sat and smoked and watched the activity. Plainclothesmen and technical people were still moving back and forth, going upstairs and returning. The front door kept opening and closing, giving blinding semaphores of sunlight. I saw Donlon twice more, once talking with a group of plainclothesmen that included one of the two that had questioned me, once with two others interrogating Padbury.

After about fifteen minutes a thin guy in a short-sleeved white shirt, needing a haircut, came over to me and said, "What do you think?"

"I don't," I said.

"Understand it was a girl killed them," he said.

I looked at him. "You press?"

"That's me. You want to see my card? I got an okay at the door."

"I'm a citizen," I said. "You want to talk to one of the other fellas."

He started to grin, as though I were kidding him, but then he saw I was serious, and he frowned instead. "You ain't a dick?"

"Where'd you get that word from? The funnies?"

He pointed at me. "You're a cop," he said.

"Wrong. What did they find upstairs?"

"What are you asking me for?"

"Because I don't know."

He kept studying me and studying me, trying to figure me out. Finally he said, "Two stiffs."

"Who?"

"One male, vanilla. One female, chocolate."

I said, "What's that supposed to mean?"

"Integration," he said. "A white guy and a spade chick, both cut up with the same knife. How come you're sitting here and you ain't a cop and you don't know anything?"

"I happened to be here."

"You hang out in this kind of place all the time."

"No."

"If I don't get it from you I'll get it from somebody else."

I said, "You get it from somebody else." I knew it was stupid to antagonize him, but I couldn't help it. It wasn't in me to tell my story any more. Besides, he'd get the background from somebody else anyway, there was no way to cover that. I'd made the papers in a small way when I was thrown off the force, and now if this homicide was juicy enough there'd probably be a rehash of it all in the tabloids. It sounded juicy enough.

Where had the female Negro body come from? I wished I could ask George Padbury about Negro girl friends of Terry Wilford's, past or present, but we had been separated now and it wasn't likely we'd be allowed back together. Besides, it didn't matter. I was just working from reflex, as though nothing had ever come to an end.

It felt odd to be in the bleachers.

The reporter asked me a couple more questions, but I didn't have any answers that were any use to him, so he finally went away. I saw him get into conversation with a couple plainclothesmen in the kitchen.

A few minutes later one of the two who'd questioned me came over and said, "That's all we need for now, Mr. Tobin. We've got your address, we'll probably be in touch. You going to be in town?"

"Yes," I said. "I'll be in town."

"Thank you for your cooperation," he said. His face and voice and eyes were blank.

"You're welcome," I said. I got up and went out to the bright humid sunlight, and a news photographer snapped my picture in an offhand fashion. I suppose he thought I was one of the investigating officers.

A small semicircle of spectators stood around on the sidewalk, perspiring. Most of them wore sunglasses. They looked hot and uncomfortable, but they didn't move. I stepped through them, and walked over to Sixth Avenue and Fourth Street and took my subway out to Queens.

Kate met me at the door, saying, "How did it go?"

"Bad. Have you got any iced coffee?"

"I can make some. Come on out to the kitchen. What happened?"

We went out to the kitchen, and I sat where Robin had sat yesterday, and while Kate made iced coffee I told her what had happened. She listened in silence for the most part, only once turning and looking at me and saying, "Oh, Mitch." As though I were the one she felt sorry for.

As I was finishing, the phone rang. Kate went out to the hall to answer it, and came back to say, "It's a reporter." She sounded worried.

I said, "Tell him I'm out. You don't know anything."

"All right," she said. She started away.

I said after her, "Then you'd better leave it off the hook."

7

I KNOW how to live under siege. I did it once before, when I was dropped from the force. You don't answer the telephone. You don't answer the doorbell. You don't leave the house. You get some neighbor or friend to do your grocery shopping for you, you send your teen-age son Bill off to spend a few days with relatives on Long Island, and you wait for everything to quiet down. It always does, eventually.

The siege was short-lived, this time. It lasted through Sunday and part of Monday, but by Monday afternoon it was over. No one was interested in me for Tuesday's paper.

It was too hot to go outside anyway, so I wouldn't have been working on my wall even if there'd been no siege. I spent the time in my office upstairs, an unfinished room I'd started to convert from a bedroom several years ago. I was rereading Mark Twain these days, and was currently on my way through *Life on the Mississippi*. I've always been a reader, but lately I seem to limit myself to pre-twentieth-century authors. I have no interest in writing that reminds me of my own world. And I never any more read newspapers or magazines.

When the doorbell rang late Monday afternoon I thought it was probably a reporter again, making one last effort, but then I heard

Kate go to the door, and voices, so it had to be someone else. I stayed where I was. There was no one I particularly wanted to see.

The voices receded to the living room, and I spent the next five minutes not quite reading my book. My eyes were on the page, but my concentration was in my ears, listening for Kate's tread on the stairs. I read the same paragraph over and over.

It took five minutes and then I heard her coming. I closed the book, tossed it onto the desk, and sat there waiting. If it wasn't a reporter, it more or less had to be the police.

But when Kate came in I could see by her expression it was something else. She said, "It's Rita Gibson. Rita Kennely. Robin's mother."

"She wants me to tell her about it?"

"They arrested Robin," she said. "This afternoon, at the hospital."

I nodded. "I knew they would."

"You knew?"

"She's guilty, Kate." I spread my hands. "There was nobody up there but her. Nobody alive. Nobody came down after her."

Kate said, "You can't believe that girl did a bloody thing like that. Killed those two people. She couldn't have, Mitch. You saw the girl, you know that as well as I do. It wasn't in her. She couldn't have done it."

"Nobody else could have done it," I said. "And *you* know as well as *I* do that anybody is capable of anything. I learned that in my years on the force." The unstated added sentence was: And I'm a prime example myself.

If Kate was aware of that unspoken addition she didn't show it. She said, "Mitch, I don't believe Robin Kennely killed anybody, and you don't believe it either."

"I don't believe anything," I said. "I'm not thinking about it."

"That's the absolute truth. If you *did* think about it, you'd know that girl is innocent."

"I'm not going to think about it," I said. "It doesn't matter what I know or what I think. I'm not a part of it."

"It matters to *her*," Kate said fiercely, gesturing at the doorway. "It matters to Robin's mother. You owe her that much, Mitch, you can at least talk to her."

"What am I supposed to say? That her daughter did kill two people? That her daughter didn't kill two people? There's nothing I can say to her, Kate, there's nothing I can do but sit there in front of her and be miserable. I'd rather be miserable up here."

"Mitch, you can't refuse to *see* the woman."

"I can," I said. "I have to. I'm not involved. I'm not going to get involved. It costs too much. I went out yesterday to help, and look what it turned into."

"Mitch—"

"I don't owe Rita Gibson a thing," I said. "And I'm not going to start anything, I'm not going to let anything start around me."

She spread her hands, saying, "What do you mean, start? What could start?"

"Do something. That's what she'll say, and then you'll start saying it too. Do something. Robin Kennely didn't kill anybody, so go on out and talk to people, nose around, do this, do that, find out who really did the killings."

"Nobody's asking you to do anything like that, Mitch."

"Not yet," I said. "But soon they will. She will, and then you will."

"Mitch, what if that girl is found guilty?"

"Kate, what if she is guilty?"

"But she isn't! Won't you at least listen? Read the newspaper stories about it, listen to the girl's mother."

"I'm not going out there," I said. "I'm staying in here. And I'm not talking to anybody about anything, I'm not thinking about anything. I'm staying in here, and one day is the same as the next."

She studied me, trying to find some way through, and then she said, "Is it really this important to you?"

"Yes."

She spread her hands. "Then there's nothing I can say."

She turned away, and I said, "I'm sorry, Kate. I just can't, that's all."

She nodded, not looking at me.

I said, "If they've made a mistake, they'll find it themselves. They usually do."

"Yes," she said, and went out of the room.

I listened to the sound of her going down the stairs, and then I listened to the murmuring silence. They were in the living room, too far away to really be heard except as a vague background murmur, rising and falling.

But what else could I do? Any action I might take would be futile, pointless. To talk to the woman downstairs would require thinking about yesterday, which was not only futile but also painful and which I didn't want to do. And besides, it is true that most police mistakes are discovered and rectified before a trial is reached. The exception gets the publicity, but it gets the publicity because it is the exception.

I picked up *Life on the Mississippi* and opened to my page, but didn't manage to read. I sat there, and waited, and after a long interval I heard voices, and then the sound of the front door. I waited for Kate to come upstairs, but she didn't, and after a while I began to read again, finished that paragraph for the last time, turned the page, and went on.

Kate came up an hour or so later, just a minute after I'd heard the phone ring down there. She came to the doorway and said, "It's George Padbury. He says it's important."

"No," I said.

"I told him I didn't think you would," she said. There was no accusation in her face or voice. She went out of the doorway and started again down the stairs.

I got to my feet, left the room, stopped at the head of the stairs. I called her name, and she stopped and looked up at me. I said, "If it is cowardice, it's still necessary to me."

"I know," she said, and abruptly her face softened. "It's all right, Mitch," she said. "I do understand."

"I'll come downstairs awhile," I said.

We went down together to the first floor, and she picked up the phone, listened, and said, "He didn't wait. He's hung up." She cradled the phone and smiled at me, saying, "He solved the problem for us."

He hadn't—no one ever would—but I smiled back and said, "Good."

8

THE NEXT day, Tuesday, at about four-thirty in the afternoon, the doorbell rang. I was in the living room, watching an Errol Flynn pirate movie on television, and I got at once to my feet.

Kate passed through on her way from the kitchen, and said as she went by, "It's all right, you can stay there. I won't let anyone in."

"Good." I remained on my feet, near the television set, watching the living-room doorway and listening above the background music of the movie for the sounds of voices at the door. Bill was back from Long Island today, at the moment up in his room at work on one of his mysterious projects, and this could conceivably be someone for him.

When Kate came back a minute later, she looked troubled, and two men in suits came in after her. She said, "They're detectives, Mitch."

I looked at them, trying to see in their faces if they knew about me, but they were both impassive. They were youngish men, very neat but slightly burly. One of them said, "We'd like you to come along with us, Mr. Tobin, if you have the time."

I said, "What's the problem?"

"No problem. Just a portion of your statement on the Wilford case we'd like to go over with you."

"Why can't you do it here?"

The other one said, in a reasonable voice, "The captain wants to talk to you, Mr. Tobin. It won't take long, and we'll bring you right back here."

I felt a grim familiarity, listening to him. Those same assurances had come calmly from my own mouth at one time, and I felt my hackles rise slightly at the echo now returning. When I had given such assurances, sometimes they had been true and sometimes they had been tactical lies aimed at bringing a potentially dangerous person into custody with the least trouble and fuss.

Surely this time it was the truth. There was no reason to suspect me of being a potentially dangerous person, and looking at these two I could see from the bored calmness of their manner that they had no such suspicion. But why bring me in? It might merely be to give me a little bit of a bad time, just on general principles. In any case, there was nothing to do but go along with them and see what happened.

I said, "I'll have to put on shoes. They're upstairs."

"Of course."

They didn't accompany me upstairs, which was another sign that I wasn't under any particular current cloud. I made it as fast as I could, wanting to get the thing over with, taking only enough time to put on my shoes and change to a less wrinkled shirt.

They were waiting near the front door when I came down. I told Kate I would either be home within the hour or would call her, and then the three of us left the house.

Their car was a green Mercury. I said, "Back or front?"

One of them said, "You might as well ride in back."

They both got into the front seat, and we started off.

The one who wasn't driving turned and grinned at me over his shoulder and said, "You didn't have to make time limits with your wife. We really will bring you back."

"Good," I said.

"What does she do, if you don't show up in an hour?"

"Starts making phone calls," I said.

He nodded. "That's what I thought. I hear you used to be on the force."

"That's right."

He kept looking at me, smiling, waiting for me to say something more, which meant he didn't yet know the story. He wouldn't hear it now, either, not from me; when the silence between us became awkward I turned my head away and watched the buildings go by the side window, and that was the end of conversation in the car.

The precinct, when we got to it, was an old brick building with slate steps, flanked by a tailor shop on one side and a grim-looking public school on the other. We double-parked by a fire plug and they brought me in, both of them much cooler toward me now. They escorted me up to the second floor, told me to wait on a bench in the hall there, and went through a door with DETECTIVE SQUAD on the frosted glass.

It had been a long while since I'd been in a place like this, and I found its sense of distorted familiarity more unsettling than I would have suspected. There was no comfort for me in the old wood of the bench, the walls painted two unlovely shades of green, the dark oiled wooden floor, the ceiling with its cream-colored paint peeling in one corner. As I sat there alone and waited, I found myself getting increasingly nervous and agitated, till at last I had to get to my feet and pace up and down the hall to work off the tension. I tried to hold my movements to a casual stroll but kept going instead at a faster and faster stride, then abruptly breaking it back to the stroll and building all over again, so that I'm sure I must have looked like a rookie out there practicing how to walk a beat.

It was only a few minutes I waited, but it seemed an hour. The same two detectives came out, and the one who'd tried to chat with me in the car said, "Captain Linther wants to see you now." He was still cold, because of the way I'd acted before.

I got to my feet and they led me through the bullpen, a long bleak room lined with small square wooden desks, each with its telephone, most now unoccupied. One man in shirt sleeves was pecking at an old typewriter in the corner, another at one of the desks was murmuring into a phone.

At the far end was the door marked CAPTAIN. They didn't come in with me, but stood aside for me to enter and then shut the door after me.

I was now in a small square office done in the same color scheme as the hall. A large wooden desk, scrupulously neat but battered by age, dominated the room. The other furniture—sofa, wooden chairs, table—all were the same ancient vintage, except for a gleaming new gray metal filing cabinet in the corner. On the walls were framed photographs of the President, the current Mayor, and other less recognizable faces.

Two men were in the room, both seated, both in civilian clothing, both in their fifties. The one on the sofa was lean and rangy, with thick gray hair and a heavily lined pale face. The one behind the desk—this would be Captain Linther—was a balding bulky man who obviously *had* heard the story of my being thrown off the force; he looked at me with apparent distaste and said, "So you're Tobin."

I said nothing, because there was nothing to say.

He turned his head to the side, saying, "This is Captain Driscoll, Twenty-seventh Squad."

I said, "How do you do?" and Captain Driscoll nodded.

Captain Linther said, "Captain Driscoll wants to talk to you about a murder case in his precinct you're involved in." He turned his head again, said, "Well, he's all yours," and got to his feet. "I'll be down the hall."

Captain Driscoll thanked him, waited till Captain Linther was out of the office, and then looked at me and said, "Sit down, Tobin."

"Thank you." I sat on a wooden chair not far from him.

He took out a pipe and a dark leather pouch. Watching his

hands fill the pipe, he said, "You're a witness in that double killing in my precinct."

"I was there, yes."

He glanced at me, then back at pouch and pipe. "Why were you there?"

"Robin Kennely asked me to come. She's a relative of mine, second cousin."

"Why did she ask you?" He put the pouch away and looked at me directly.

I said, "A plainclothesman had been giving her friends at that coffee house a bad time. They didn't know if he wanted to be bought or what, so she asked me to have a talk with him."

He nodded heavily, and put the pipe in his mouth, and began to pat himself for matches. "I still have one question in my mind," he said.

I took matches from my pocket and extended them to him. Because he wanted me to, I asked, "What's that?"

"Thank you," he said, taking the matches. He lit one, and between puffs on his pipe he said, "It seems to me, you're accusing, one of my men, of trying to get a bribe." He shook the match out, leaned forward to drop it into an ashtray on Captain Linther's desk, sat back and looked at me again. "Do you have any evidence to back up this accusation?"

"I should have known," I said.

He looked puzzled. "You should have known what?"

"I've been away from the force too long," I said. "Otherwise I'd have realized you'd have to come to me for this. I'd have realized a captain wouldn't be here to ask questions on a murder case."

"I'm not sure I follow you," he said. He'd taken the pipe from his mouth and was holding it in his hand, where it was in danger of going out. My matches were still in his other hand.

I said, "Let me go over my statement again."

"I don't see why that would be necessary."

"It won't take long."

He shrugged, noticed he was holding my matches, and leaned forward to give them back to me.

"Thank you," I said. "Robin Kennely told me there was a plain-clothesman who'd told her friends there were some violations in their coffee house they had to take care of. They weren't entirely sure what they were supposed to do, so she asked me to have a talk with the plainclothesman and find out."

He frowned at me. "Are you changing your story?"

"It's a change of interpretation, that's all," I said. "Do you want me to dictate it?"

It was too fast for him, he wasn't being given a chance to get everything covered neatly with rationalizations. He said, "Your original statement accused Detective Donlon of attempted extortion. Now you want to change your statement. Was that earlier statement a lie?"

"Not at all," I said. "I stand by every word in it. But I can see now where it might be misleading, so I want to make an amended statement that you can put in place of the original one."

"If you have evidence of wrongdoing on my squad," he said, "you can bring it forward. I'm not covering for anybody."

"I have no evidence," I said.

"Then it seems to me," he said, "your original statement may be actionable."

"No. I only repeated hearsay, what I'd been told by Robin Kennely. I have never stated whether I believed or disbelieved her."

"Do you believe her?"

"I have no opinion."

We disliked each other intensely by now, and neither of us was bothering to hide it. His pipe had gone out, still held in his right hand. He said, "Have you always been this cynical, Tobin? Or are you just bitter against the force?"

"I know how the world works," I said. "I don't think you want to push me back to my old statement."

He hesitated, and I knew what was bothering him. He'd come

here to get something, and he'd gotten it too easily. He'd expected to have to browbeat me into changing my statement about Donlon, instead of which I'd volunteered to do it before he'd gotten the question well asked. He was on a seamy task, and we both knew it, and I had agreed so readily that now we were perforce on the same team, accomplices, and he disliked the idea of being my accomplice in anything.

Still, there was nothing he could do about it. He shook his head heavily, and looked at his unlit pipe, and then back at me, saying, "You want to make an amended statement."

"Naturally."

"I'll arrange for a stenographer," he said, and got reluctantly to his feet.

"Thank you," I said, trying to make it pointed, trying to rub his nose in the fact that he should be thanking me.

He went out without a word.

I had no doubt that Captain Driscoll was personally honest. If indeed I were to bring him direct and irrefutable evidence that Detective Edward Donlon was demanding bribes, I don't doubt that Captain Driscoll would go after Donlon all the way. On the other hand, I don't doubt but that Captain Driscoll already knew everybody on his squad who was square and everybody who was bent, knew in a silent and unofficial way, and was prepared to let the world go on behaving in its normal manner just so long as no one caused any trouble.

In the present case, the double murder at Thing East, what he had was a straightforward homicide, complete with suspect in custody, into which my statement intruded the unwelcome and irrelevant specter of police corruption. If he could get me to alter my statement in a way that had nothing to do with the murder, so much the better.

Of course, he would have preferred it to have happened much more subtly than I had permitted. But I was tired, I was impatient with his grubby esprit de corps, and I disliked everything about the atmosphere of this building. I didn't want to play games here, I wanted merely to do what was required of me and then go home.

The stenographer came in a few minutes later, a skinny uniformed patrolman with thick glasses. He sat at the desk and took my statement, doing his shorthand with crabbed concentration. When I was done, he said, "This won't take long," and left.

Hard on his heels Captain Linther returned. Still looking at me with an expression of repugnance on his face, he said, "Captain Driscoll's done with you now. You can wait outside."

I went out to the bullpen and sat at a handy empty desk. The man who had been typing was still there, but the one who had been on the phone was gone. Two other desks were now occupied, though, the man at one of them filling out forms with a ballpoint pen, the other one eating a sandwich, drinking a container of coffee, and reading the *Daily News*.

The feeling of familiarity here was stronger than ever, though the physical similarities between this place and the squadroom of the precinct where I'd been assigned were few. Still, the aura was the same, so much so that when the phone rang I looked around the room to see if it was my turn to catch the squeal. Then, embarrassed, I looked down at my hands in my lap, hoping no one had seen my move or comprehended it. I stayed in that position until the stenographer came back with the typed copies of my new statement. I signed them all, and he took them into the captain's office. I continued to wait.

Captain Linther came out of his office and walked over to stand in front of me. Standing, he seemed shorter and bulkier than he had while seated behind his desk. He said, "One thing I want to say to you, Tobin, before you go."

I waited.

"I didn't know you lived in my precinct," he said. "Not till now. I don't like the idea you living in my precinct. If you're smart, you'll keep your head down."

"I will," I said.

"That's all," he said. "You can go now."

"I was told I'd be driven back."

"I can't spare the men," he said, and turned away, and walked back to his office.

I took a cab.

9

KATE met me at the door, saying, "There's someone here to see you, Mitch."

By the expression on her face I knew I wasn't going to like it and she was going to try to persuade me to do something I didn't want to do. Not moving any farther into the house, keeping out of range of the living-room doorway, I said, "Who is it?"

"A boy named Hulmer Fass. He was another partner in the coffee house."

"I don't want to see him, Kate. I'm not having anything to do with any of that."

"Mitch—"

"No," I said. I went past her, quickly past the living-room doorway, and started up the stairs.

Behind me, she said, "Mitch, George Padbury is dead."

I stopped. I looked back down at her. "How?"

"Hit and run. Thirty minutes after he called here yesterday. Died in the hospital this morning, without regaining consciousness."

I frowned, and gripped the banister. I didn't want to be involved. "It doesn't have to connect," I said.

"Mitch," she said.

"What do the police say?"

"What you say. No connection."

"They're closer to it than we are," I said.

"No, they aren't," said another voice, and standing in the living-room doorway was a light-skinned Negro boy of about twenty, tall and slender and economical and neat, narrowly dressed in a dark latest-style suit. "They're spectators," he said. "We're standing in it."

"Not me," I told him. "I have no connection with anything. I don't know you, I don't want to know you."

"Mitch!"

I turned back to Kate. "I was just told by a captain of detectives," I said, "to keep my head down. That's what I intend to do."

The Negro boy—Hulmer Fass, Kate had said his name was—said to me, "The reason I came here, Mr. Tobin, is because I figured we're in this together. You and me, we're locked in."

"I don't see that."

"We don't know yet why he hit George," he said. "If it's because he's connected to the joint, then I'm next. If it's because he was there when it happened, you're next."

Kate said, "Mitch, you can't stay out of it. What if he comes after you?"

"I'll worry about that when it happens," I said.

Kate said, "What about George Padbury?"

"What about him? He's dead."

"Thirty minutes after you refused to talk to him."

I raised my hand. "No," I said. "You can't do that."

Hulmer Fass shook his head. "That's how it goes with noninvolvement, Mr. Tobin," he said. "One day it's not your problem, the next day they're all over you."

"I'm not responsible for George Padbury's death," I said.

He gave me a smile of knowing and cynical contempt. "Goodbye, baby," he said, and turned toward the door.

Kate said to him, "No, wait. Don't go yet." She looked up at me. "You go on upstairs, Mitch," she said, "and think it out. You think about Robin, in Bellevue, going to be transferred to jail. You think about George Padbury and this boy here and your own family. When you've got it all thought out, you'll find us in the kitchen." To the boy she said, "Come along, Hulmer. Do you like iced coffee?"

He was grinning at her respectfully. "Sure thing," he said, and they walked back to the kitchen together.

I didn't go up to the second floor. I sat down where I was, on the stairs, and felt the iron hand closing on me. But all I wanted was to stay here, stay in my hole, keep my head down.

Bill came thundering into the house as I sat there. Fourteen years old, he was well into the transition from open childhood to the mysterious complexity of the young people connected with places like Thing East. How much of my disgrace he knew about I had never learned, nor tried to learn. There was a widening rift between my son and me, caused for the most part I knew by myself, but there was nothing I could do to mend it without opening myself, which I didn't ever want to do.

Now he came bounding up the stairs, a brown paper bag in his hand, and paused beside me to say, "What's up, Dad?"

"Thinking," I said. "What've you got there?"

"Tubes," he said. "See you."

"See you."

He pounded on up, leaving me alone. I shook my head, and got to my feet, and went down to the kitchen, where I said to Hulmer Fass, sitting at the kitchen table, "Do you know how to get in touch with George Padbury's brother? The almost lawyer?"

"Ralph? Sure."

"We'll need him. Would you call him?"

He got to his feet. "To come out here?"

"Yes."

He smiled. "Yes, sir."

I said, "Is there anybody else connected with Thing East? Any more partners?"

"Two," he said. "You want them?"

"Yes. The phone's in the hall."

"When do you want them?"

"As soon as possible."

"Done," he said, and went out to make the calls.

I looked at Kate and said, "Don't grin at me. I want you to know I hate this, I intend to get it over with as quick as I can, and when it's done I'll go straight back into my box."

"It's all right, Mitch," she said. "Really. It's all right." Which only meant she didn't want to believe I was telling her the truth.

10

WE WERE all assembled by quarter to seven, six of us sitting around the living room, the coolest place in the house. Outside the sun was still strong, refusing to give way to twilight. Inside, the feeling of twilight, muted and forlorn, was a heavy aura around us.

Hulmer Fass had stayed to dinner, during which he and Bill had gotten into a complex electronic discussion in which it emerged that one of the things Bill was working on up in his room was a homemade phonograph, using odd parts from here and there. Hulmer did more talking with Bill in the course of that one meal than I'd done all told for a year, and I listened with agonized embarrassment at the degree of my hunger for knowledge of my son. I envied Hulmer his easy access to Bill, knew the envy was absurd to the point of irrationality, and envied him anyway.

After dinner Hulmer and I moved to the living room and engaged in uneasy conversation. Neither of us was sure of his attitude toward the other, so that we spoke haltingly on the safest of topics—weather and highways and baseball—skirting even around the subject that had brought us together. As each of the others arrived, Hulmer made introductions and then the new member joined our uncomfortable group. After Kate had the dishes done, and joined us, talk was somewhat easier, but still hampered by the reason for our all being here.

Ralph Padbury was the first arrival, and simultaneously looked exactly like his dead brother and nothing at all like him. Where George Padbury had taken the basic features common to both brothers and overlaid them with long hair, bushy mustache, and turtleneck sweater, Ralph Padbury had chosen a severe, pedestrian, anonymous, clerkish façade, with slicked-down hair, clean-shaven face, low-priced conservative suit and shirt and tie, and bookish horn-rim glasses. He seemed incomplete without an attaché case.

He also looked unnaturally pale, having that pinched chalky expresson about the eyes that means a recent severe shock. His brother had died a scant twelve hours before, and it showed in his face.

A girl named Vicki Oppenheim was next. Short and stout, she was dressed all in black—sweater, skirt, stockings, shoes—and had to be dying of the heat, but didn't show it. Her hair was black and long, gathered with a red rubber band at the back of her head and then falling free to below her shoulders. Her face was rather pretty, in a chubby way. Her natural expression was obviously an ebullient smile, which she was trying with uncertain success to banish, due to the seriousness of the occasion.

"Golly," she said, when Hulmer introduced us. "I don't know what to say. Golly."

Kate saved me, saying to the girl, "None of us knows what to say, Vicki. Come sit over here."

The last to show up was a boy named Abe Selkin, thin, intense, hot-eyed, spade-bearded, crackling with intelligence and energy. He scanned the room with a quick computer-like glance and said, "War council."

"Not war," I said. "Defense."

He nodded briskly, studied me for a millisecond, and said, "You're in charge."

"Not the way you mean," I said. "I'm not putting an army together here, I have no tasks to be performed. What I want from you people is enough information to make it possible for me to act on my own."

"We're part of the scene," Selkin said. "You could use us."

"Perhaps," I lied. "For now, I only want information. Would you sit over there with Hulmer?"

"Right."

I went back to my own chair before saying, "I've done my best to stay out of this thing. Which means I haven't even read the newspaper stories about it. I know almost nothing, so forgive me if I ask what may seem like stupid questions. Like the name of the murdered girl, I don't know that."

There was silence, each of them obviously waiting for one of the others to answer me, until Kate volunteered, saying, "Her name was Irene Boles, Mitch."

"Irene Boles." I had armed myself with a notebook, into which I wrote the name. I looked at Hulmer. "What was her connection with the group?"

He grinned a little and shook his head. "None," he said.

"None? Who was she?"

"Hooker," he said. "From uptown."

Abe Selkin said, "According to the papers, she was a prostitute, she'd done time."

"Where did she live?"

Hulmer answered me, still with the same faint grin: "Harlem."

"And none of you had ever seen her before?"

They all shook their heads, and Kate said, "The newspaper said she usually spent her time in the midtown area."

I said, "Would Terry Wilford have been likely to know her professionally?"

"Not a chance," Abe Selkin said.

Vicki Oppenheim, looking wide-eyed and innocent, said, "Terry didn't have to pay for it, Mr. Tobin."

"All right," I said. "How about socially? Could he have met her somehow in her non-working life?"

Hulmer said, "Terry didn't know that chickie. She was a snowhead; if she wasn't on Broadway working she was up in her place in Harlem stoned to the eyes."

I said, "Is that a guess? Kate, did the papers say she was a dope addict?"

She nodded. "It said she was under the influence when she died."

"All right." I looked from face to face. "I need a truthful answer to this one," I said. "It won't go any farther than this room."

"We know that," Abe Selkin said.

"Was Terry Wilford an addict?"

Selkin shook his head. "Definitely not."

"Are any of the rest of you?"

"That stupid we're not," Selkin said.

Hulmer said, "We aren't users, Mr. Tobin, that's straight."

"What about George Padbury?"

The brother, Ralph Padbury, who until now had been sitting quietly in his chair and seeming too dazed to really comprehend the conversation going on around him, suddenly sat up, very angry, and said, "My brother never touched any of that stuff! Who do you think you are?"

"I'm sorry," I said. "I have to ask all the questions, I have to know where I stand."

"My brother's *dead,* don't you realize that?"

Vicki Oppenheim reached out and took Padbury's hand, saying, "Come on, Ralph. Everybody knows, that's why we're here. Mr. Tobin isn't putting George down, he's just trying to get the picture."

"He can just leave George out of this."

Vicki shook her head. "No, he can't. He has to know everything about George. And about me, and Abe, and Hully. And you, too."

Padbury pulled his hand free, saying, "I have nothing to do with any of this. I told you people at the outset, I'm not involved, I'm not a party to any of this. I have my own—I have to take—"

"I know how you feel, Mr. Padbury," I said. "I feel much the same way myself. But a situation is—"

"*My* life *isn't* ruined!" he said hotly, glaring at me. "What does it matter to you, what do you care what happens? Or any of the rest of you? What sort of, what sort of *reputations* do you have to—I have a future to think about, a career."

"Mr. Padbury," I said, and the doorbell rang. Kate got to her feet, and I went on, "No one is here to accuse anybody of anything, or muddy anybody's reputation. I have to know the situation, that's all."

"Well, I'm out of it!" he said, and got to his feet, moving with the jittery agitation of an essentially mild man driving himself to violent reaction. "I don't know why you people called me here, I —Hulmer, I told you on the phone I didn't see what good I could do, and—"

I said, "Mr. Padbury, did you know Irene Boles?"

"What?" Thrown off stride, he blinked at me without comprehension. "Who?"

"The dead woman."

"The pros— *No!*"

"I didn't think so," I said. "But you do know Robin Kennely."

"Of course I know Robin. Everybody in this room knows her."

"She's in jail," I said.

"Bellevue," Hulmer corrected me, and added, "But it's the same thing."

Padbury said, "There's nothing I can do for her. I know what you're trying to say, but there's just nothing I can do to help her." He had calmed down in spite of himself, and went on reasonably, "I understand her parents are fairly well-to-do, I imagine they have hired attorneys to represent her. If she's innocent, I'm sure—"

Abe Selkin said, "Come off it, Ralph. Do you think she killed George?"

"All right." Padbury nodded, impatiently conceding the point, and said, "But the fact remains, I can do nothing to help her."

"You can help me," I said, "and I'm trying to help her."

"What can you do that—?"

"Mitch."

I turned my head, and Kate was in the doorway, and standing beside her, looking from face to face with a faint grim smile on his lips, was Detective Edward Donlon, the cop who had started all this.

"Quite a gathering," Donlon said, and took one step into the room. "What's the occasion?"

11

I GOT to my feet. "You wanted to see me?"

"I'm happy to see all you people," Donlon said. He looked at Ralph Padbury, frowned at him, finally said, "Who are you, boy? You look familiar."

"He's my guest," I said. "Kate, would you stay with our guests? Mr. Donlon and I will talk in the kitchen."

"You know who I am."

"You were pointed out to me."

"Who did that nice thing?"

"George Padbury."

His eyes flickered, and then he looked at Ralph Padbury again. "That's who you look like," he said.

I walked across the living room, saying, "Come along. We can talk in the kitchen."

"Why don't we stay here?" he said. "Don't let me interrupt, you people just go right on like before. Talk about whatever you were talking about when I came in. What was the subject, Fass?"

I said, "Donlon, are you here to create a situation?"

He looked at me, amused and mock-innocent. That heavy jaw, bluish-gray now and almost in need of a razor, was deceptive, distracting from the quick intelligence in the eyes. Donlon looked almost like a dumb bull, but not quite. He was smart, and he wouldn't act without a reason.

He said, "What's the problem, Tobin? This is a friendly call, a bunch of your new friends getting together. I mean, these people aren't *old* friends of yours, are they?"

I said, "Excuse me," and started around him, toward the hall doorway.

"Where you going? Aren't you the host?"

"I'm calling Captain Driscoll," I said. "Maybe he'll tell me what you're here for."

"That's enough, Tobin," he said, and his voice was suddenly all steel.

I turned and looked at him. "We're in my house, Donlon," I said. "In my house I decide what's enough and who talks to who and when people come and go. Is this an official call?"

"I already said it wasn't."

"If you want to talk to me," I said, "we'll talk privately. In the kitchen. You coming? Or do you want to leave?"

He didn't like it. He wanted to throw some weight around—not so much because of me as because of the presence of the coffee-house crowd—and he couldn't do it. I had the edge here, and it bothered him, the way a man might be bothered by too-tight shoes.

But he didn't let the silence get too long. He shrugged, and smiled, and kept looking directly at me as he said, "Well, that's all right, I'll be happy to come to the kitchen with you, Tobin. I can talk with these other folk some other time."

"That's right. Come along." I turned away again, and left the living room, and walked down the hall to the kitchen, hearing him come along behind me. From the living room there was total silence.

At the kitchen entrance I stood aside and let Donlon go through first, then I followed and pushed shut the swinging door. It was perhaps the second time in fifteen years that door had been closed.

I said, "Sit down if you want."

But he didn't want. He turned to face me and he was all cold now, all steel. He said, "What are you mixing into, Tobin? What are you and those brats brewing?"

"You're beginning to sound official again," I told him.

"You got trouble enough," he said. "You want to stay out of the way."

I said, "What are you worried about? Don't you know Driscoll had me in to see him today?"

He hadn't known it. His eyes narrowed, and the hands closed into fists at his sides. He said, "What about, Tobin?"

"My statement. He didn't like it, so I changed it."

He wasn't sure he understood me. Warily he said, "Changed it how?"

I said, "My cousin Robin Kennely told me a police officer had told her friends about violations at Thing East. They weren't sure what they were supposed to do to correct these violations, and Robin wanted me to talk to the police officer and find out what was required."

The wariness eased out of his expression and he made a small happy smile, saying, "What do you know? That's what he wanted, huh?"

"That's what I gave him."

"And then he was happy?"

"He was satisfied."

"That's good." His smile widened and he nodded, saying, "That was smart, Tobin, very smart. You don't rock the boat."

"I remember the drill," I said.

The smile went away, replaced by a frown. "I don't follow you, Tobin," he said. "First you do a smart thing with Driscoll, and then you do something dumb."

"Like what?"

"Like having that crowd in your living room. They're trouble-makers, Tobin. Dumbheads. Smart-ass kids. Bo-*hee*-mians. You going to be scoutmaster for them? You know the type they are, you must of run into them yourself back in the old days."

I knew what he meant. Any large city, and most particularly New York City, attracts hordes of the rootless young, youths who have left home as part of a vague unfocused revolt against authority—and, I suppose, against the inevitability of their future —and who, with too much time and too little money, become bored and restless and itchy, spoiling for any sort of action. Whether it's drugs or sex or political activism or just ordinary barroom brawling, many of these youngsters come to the attention of the police sooner or later, and their attitude toward the cop is a distillation of their attitude toward home and parents. The cop is the bluntest and most direct symbol of authority, that authority against which the youth is already in rebellion. Professional criminals are less trouble to arresting officers than are members of the cult of rebellious youth.

But if the youngsters right now in my living room did bear some resemblance to that type, and if they undoubtedly traveled with a group that contained several members of the type, and if they would react to arrest or police harassment in the same way as members of the type, it was still true that they themselves were other than or more than the type. Vicki Oppenheim, with only minor changes of dress—and, probably, speech—would fit right in at any rural church picnic in the country. Abe Selkin was too direct and self-contained to be involved with anything as vague as revolt against authority. Hulmer Fass, even more self-contained, was an entire population in and of himself, too completely divorced from the world to allow anything in it to upset him emotionally. And Ralph Padbury, of course, didn't even bear a similarity to the bo-hee-mians, to use Donlon's word.

But whether Donlon was right or wrong about them was irrelevant and beside the point, the point being that their presence in my living room was no concern of his, which I told him, saying, "What are they to you? They can be where they want to be. I can have in my house who I want in my house."

"You aren't sitting around," he said, "playing spin the bottle. They're up to something, and they want you in on it. Am I right?"

"What would they be up to? I already told you the amended statement I gave your captain. You have nothing to fear from me, and nothing to fear from those people in there either."

"Then why are they here?"

"That's their business," I said.

"I'm making it mine."

I shook my head, and we stood looking at one another, me disliking him for being arrogant and on the take, and him disliking me for being an unknown quantity that could cause him trouble. Finally he shrugged and said, "Why struggle? I'll get it later."

"Don't start making trouble for those children," I said.

He gave me the mock-innocent look again. "What makes you think I'd make trouble?"

"We had some like you in my old precinct," I said.

He didn't like that. He said, "We don't have any like you, Tobin. We like it that way."

Simple insults don't bother me any more, so I said, "Just remember to leave them alone."

"Or?"

"Or I see if I can make trouble for you."

He frowned at me, not sure of himself, and said, "You think you can? With your past history, you think you can make trouble for anybody?"

"I don't know. I can try. I still know a couple of people. I could do my best to make a smell in your area."

Frowning, he turned away from me, walked around the kitchen table, stood facing the refrigerator for a minute. I heard him say under his breath, "Everything cuts twelve ways." Then he rubbed a hand across his face, as though he were tired, and shook himself like a dog coming out of water.

The swinging door pushed open, startling the both of us, and Bill walked in, absorbed in something inside his own head. He stopped two paces into the room and blinked at us. "I'm sorry,

Dad," he said, "I didn't know anybody was here. I thought you were all in the living room."

Donlon looked at Bill like a man seeing a long-lost relative. "Your father and I just had some private talk to do, son," he said, his voice unusually soft. "But we're just about done."

"I've just got to get a couple tools," Bill said. He went over to the tool drawer near the sink.

Donlon said, "Working on a project, eh?"

"Yes, sir." Bill got wire cutters and the smallest screwdriver out of the drawer.

"Model plane?" Donlon asked him.

"No, sir. Some phonograph stuff. Excuse me."

Donlon's eyes followed him as Bill left the room. Donlon shook his head and said, "That's when they're good. Kids, I love kids. You ever do any PAL work when you were on the force, Tobin?"

"I never seemed to have the time."

"Well, you got kids of your own. I can't have any. Thought it was Mrs. Donlon for years, but it's me. Doctor said it's me." He rubbed his face again, and it came out as hard as it had been before. "But they grow up bad," he said, "the most of them. Like that bunch you're protecting in there. The smaller kids are all right, but later on they turn bad."

"Not all of them."

"What do I care?" He gnawed on a knuckle for a second, then shook his head and said, "On this other thing, we deal."

"You'll lay off?"

He spread his hands out, palms down, and said, "Everybody floats." His eyes glinted.

I didn't trust him, there was something too sudden and electric about him, but I knew this was the best I'd be able to get from him, so I said, "Good. It's a deal."

"Now," he said, "everybody goes home." He didn't say it menacingly or like an order, but as though it followed naturally.

Which it didn't. I said, "Stop pushing."

He seemed confused for just a second, and then tightness came over his face and he said, "All right, Tobin, play your game, whatever it is. But don't show your face."

"I won't."

"Say good-bye to your guests for me," he said, and walked around me, and pushed open the swinging door.

I followed him down the hall to the front door. He opened it and went out, leaving the door ajar. I stood there in semidarkness, my hand on the knob, and watched him walk out through belated twilight to a black Plymouth parked at the curb, unmarked but obvious; he was driving an official car on his unofficial business.

When Donlon got into the Plymouth and drove away, I shut the door and went back to the living room.

12 —————————————————

THERE WAS conversation in the living room now, animated conversation, the whole group busily explaining something or other to Kate, who was nodding and smiling and not understanding a word. They were all busily and unself-consciously being themselves, without that slightly guarded overlay that people almost always put on with me. Vicki was bursting and bubbling with speech, her words tumbling over each other, she herself bouncing up and down on the couch as though she were not a fat girl; Abe Selkin was as brisk and incisive as a reform candidate's campaign manager; Hulmer was in the conversation and yet to one side of it, observant and self-aware and sympathetic and faintly amused; and Ralph Padbury, leaning slightly forward, was methodically inserting small neat footnotes into the seconds left empty by the others.

The talk trailed off as I came into the room, and everyone looked at me. I said, into the raw new silence, "It's all right, he's gone."

Abe Selkin, in his clipped way, said, "You realize he followed one of us."

"Possibly," I said.

Hulmer said, "What happens now? He hangs on our tail?"

"No. We've got a stalemate. He's to lay off us and we'll lay off him."

Hulmer smiled a thin curve of disbelief. "We lay *what* off him?"

"We don't try to make trouble for him being on the take."

Ralph Padbury, very prim, said, "It was never established that was what he wanted. We have no case there."

"I know that," I said. "But we could still raise a little dust, something that would be remembered at promotion time. It's worth it to him not to have us making a stink, even though," with a nod to Padbury, "we don't have enough to get him into a court of law."

Hulmer said, "Sounds like a shaky truce, man."

"It is." I sat down. "But it gives us a little time," I said, and picked up my notebook. Studying it, pretending the earlier flare-up with Ralph Padbury had never happened, I said, "I think we've finished with Irene Boles. Prostitute, heroin addict, no known connection with Terry Wilford or any of the rest of you." I looked up. "Has anybody found out how she got in there?"

My transition had worked; Padbury sat quiet and attentive in his chair, no longer prepared to revolt.

It was Abe Selkin who answered my question, saying, "The police theory is, Terry let her in that morning because he knew her, because they had a thing going, and she was supposed to be out of there before he got back with Robin. But she was stoned, so she didn't make it. So Terry and Robin went upstairs, Robin saw her there, and she flipped out and started slicing."

I said, "Do the police have any support for the idea that Wilford knew the girl?"

No one answered me until Kate volunteered, saying, "Nothing that's been in the paper, Mitch."

"All right." I made a note to try and check that out, and said, "Now, I'll want to talk to other people who knew Wilford. Friends and enemies, old girl friends, relatives, anybody that you four think it would be worth my while to see."

Selkin said, "What's the point?"

"Somebody murdered him," I said. "The odds are in favor of it being somebody who knew him."

Selkin said, "Why not somebody who knew the girl? The Boles girl."

"Possibly," I said. "But Wilford was murdered at home, so he's more likely to be the prime target. The murderer could also turn out to be the connecting link between the two of them, somebody who knew both Terry Wilford and Irene Boles."

With that faint smile of his, Hulmer said, "Somebody like me, maybe?"

"Maybe," I agreed. "But I don't subscribe to the theory that all Negroes know each other."

In quick succession he looked surprised, angry, and delighted, accompanying the last with laughter and saying, "Touché, man. I'll lay off."

"Good." I poised pencil over notebook. "Now I want Wilford's relatives."

Selkin said, "None local."

Vicki Oppenheim bubbled in, saying, "Nobody was really born in New York, you know. Except people like Abe and Hully, and they don't count. Terry came from Oregon, some little town in Oregon."

"All right," I said. "What about enemies?"

Vicki shook her head. "Everybody liked Terry," she started.

She would have gone on, but I've heard that paragraph from survivors before, and I didn't particularly want to hear it again, so I interrupted, saying, "No. Everybody has enemies, even the saints."

Vicki laughed, saying, "Ho-oh, nobody ever said Terry was a *saint*." Then, belatedly, it occurred to her to worry about whether she should have said something like that about someone recently dead; she put a hand over her mouth and blinked solemnly at us all.

Selkin distracted us from Vicki's embarrassment, saying, "Jack Parker, there's one."

I wrote the name down while Vicki, forgetting to be embarrassed, was saying to Selkin, "Oh, Abe, no! That was all over six months ago."

"They were never exactly buddies after that," Selkin told her.

I said, "After what?"

Selkin turned to me. "Jack was going with a bird," he said. "Terry took her away, then she went back with Jack."

I said, "What's the girl's name?"

"Ann," said Vicki. "But Jack Parker isn't mad at Terry any more, Abe, he really isn't. I mean, he wasn't. Not for *months*."

Selkin shrugged.

I said, "What's Ann's last name?"

It turned out none of them knew; she was just a girl named Ann. I said, "Do you know any way I can get in touch with her?"

"Sure," said Selkin. "She's living with Jack again. They've got a place on Sullivan Street, below Houston."

I took down the address and said, "Anybody else? Any more enemies?"

They all thought for a while, and then Hulmer said, "Well, there's always Bodkin."

Selkin frowned at him and said, "You're reaching, Hully."

Vicki leaped on that, saying, "No more than you did with Jack."

Not wanting them to disintegrate into bickering, I broke in and said, "Tell me about Bodkin."

Hulmer said, "When Terry first came to the city he roomed with this guy Bodkin. They knew each other in college or something. And Bodkin was a mooch, you know? Borrow your clothes, your booze, your bread, everything. Hang around when you're with a bird, all like that. Terry had a short once, some old Morris Minor, Bodkin took it out and racked it up on Seventh Avenue in the rain. Near that Esso station below Sheridan Square, you know? Left it there, stuck in the trunk of some parked Lincoln, some doctor's Lincoln, made Terry all kinds of grief."

Vicki said, defensively, "Terry had every right to do what he did."

"Sure he did," Hulmer said agreeably. "That isn't the point, honey."

I said, "What did he do?"

Hulmer told me, "Beat on Bodkin a little. Took Bodkin's tape recorder and some other stuff to pay for the Morris, kicked him out on the street. Bodkin tried to get the fuzz on him, so Terry stopped covering for him about the Morris, and Bodkin didn't have any license. He wound up with thirty days in the Tombs."

"What happened after that?"

Hulmer shrugged. "Nothing. Bodkin never came around any more."

Selkin said, "This all happened a year and a half ago. If Bodkin was going to make trouble he'd have done it long ago."

I said, "What's Bodkin's first name?"

"Something weird," Hulmer said. "Vicki, what was it?"

"I'm trying to think," she said, frowning mightily, and abruptly snapped her fingers and cried, "Claude!"

"Right! Claude Bodkin!" Hulmer turned to me, grinning, and said, "How's that for a name?"

"Good," I said, writing it down.

"You're one to talk," Vicki said to Hulmer.

"Hulmer Fass? What's wrong with Hulmer Fass?"

"Cut it out," Selkin told them. "This is serious."

They both sobered at once, and Hulmer almost managed to look contrite. Into their silence I said, "What about friends? Any close friends outside this group?"

"Willy Fedders," Selkin said, "but he's off in summer stock."

Vicki said, "Whatever happened to that girl Chris? Remember her?"

Hulmer said, "She married some guy in the Navy, moved out to California or some place."

Ralph Padbury, somewhat diffident, leaned forward to say, "What about Ed Regan?"

Selkin said, "Right." To me he said, "Ed's a guy lives in the building where Terry lived before he moved in over Thing East."

"What's the address?"

"On Eleventh Street, East Eleventh Street. What is it? Three-eighteen A. It's a building in back, you go through three-eighteen and it's behind there."

"Fine. Anybody else?"

They thought it over, tossed names back and forth a little, and then decided there weren't any more close friends of Wilford's in town right now. Casual acquaintances, but no one who could do me any good. So I moved on, saying, "About Thing East. Whose idea was it to begin with?"

Vicki said, "Terry. He talked to Abe about it first, didn't he, Abe?"

"He talked to George first," Selkin said. "He and George came to me, and then the three of us talked to Ralph. Well, the four of us, Robin was there, too."

Ralph Padbury leaned forward again, saying carefully, "Of course, I was never actually a partner in the enterprise. They came to me for advice about some of the legal aspects."

"I understand that. Did Terry know about the available building when he got the idea?"

Vicki said, "That's what made him think of it. Ed told him about these religious nuts, and the building, and all."

"Ed. You mean Ed Regan?"

Selkin said, "Ed's mother is in this religious group."

"All right. So Terry got the idea, and went first to George Padbury. Why him first?"

Ralph Padbury answered for his brother, saying, "George worked in a couple of coffee houses, he knew about running them."

"He was a manager?"

"No. He was a cook."

"All right. Then the two of them came to you," I said to Selkin. "Why you next?"

Selkin rubbed thumb and first finger of his right hand together.

"Money," he said. "They knew I had some money, and I'm the business type. I'm the manager."

"And Robin was there because she was Terry's girl friend, is that it?"

Vicki said, "And she's a waitress. I mean, she was. She and me, we're the waitresses."

"Who brought you in?" I asked her.

"Robin. We've been friends since way back in high school."

I turned to Hulmer. "What about you?"

"Same as Abe," he said, smiling. "I had some money. Besides, these days you've got to have a spade whatever you start up. It's token integration."

Selkin said, "Hulmer's a mechanic and a hi-fi repairman and everything else like that. He picked up all the kitchen equipment and the tables and everything, fixed everything up."

Nodding, Hulmer grinned at Selkin and said, "That, too, Abe. I'm just putting the man on. He's hip." He turned to me, saying, "Aren't you, Mr. Tobin?"

"Nobody you call mister is hip," I told him.

He laughed and said, "There you go, Abe. You see what I mean?"

I said, "Who approached you about the coffee house, Hulmer?"

"Terry," he said. "Him and George, they came to see me where I was working."

"Where was that?"

"Stereo Fixit, on Eighth Street."

"Did you people all quit your jobs for this?"

"Had to," said Selkin. "It's full-time work, opening a place like that."

"I guess it would be. All right, let's move on. Keys to the front door. I suppose each of you has a key."

"Not me," said Padbury.

"That's right, you wouldn't have. But the rest of you do."

They all nodded agreement.

I said, "Anybody else? Besides the six partners, you three and Robin and Terry and George, did anybody else have a key?"

They shook their heads, and Selkin said, "There wasn't any reason for anybody else to have a key."

I said, "What about this religious organization you rented the place from? Don't they have a key?"

"That's right!" Selkin shook his head, irritated with himself. "I'm sorry, I never even thought about that."

"Anybody else?"

This time they thought more carefully, but they finally decided no, there weren't any more keys around but the ones already mentioned, so I said, "Who do you deal with from the religious organization?"

"We go straight to the top," Hulmer told me, straight-faced. "The bishop his own self."

Selkin told me, more usefully, "Walter Johnson. Bishop Johnson, he calls himself."

"What's the religion's name?"

"New World Samaritans," Selkin said. "They're over on Avenue A now, got a store front facing the park."

"Tompkins Square Park?"

"Right."

"All right." I looked over my notes, and it seemed as though I'd covered everything I could. I said to Selkin, "Would you call Bishop Johnson and tell him I'll be coming to see him? Explain I'm on your side."

"Will do."

"And Ed Regan, too. Also, would you all give me your addresses and phone numbers before you leave? I might want to talk to one of you again later on." I looked at Hulmer, saw he was preparing a remark, and said, "For a variety of possible reasons, Hulmer."

He grinned at me. "I didn't say a word, mister."

Kate said, "Is that all now, Mitch?"

"All I can think of. Unless one of you has something I missed."

None of them did, so Kate said, "Then maybe everyone would like some refreshments. Iced tea?"

They took iced tea, and cookies, all but Ralph Padbury, who was still ill at ease to be in such nonconformist company, and who made jumbled excuses before backing hurriedly into the night. The other three stayed on, chatted with Kate much more companionably than they could possibly talk with me, and a strangely party-like aura settled over the house.

They left around eleven, all three making blanket offers of assistance, which I had no intention of taking up, and once they were gone Kate gave her opinion that all three were excellent youngsters, adding, "You don't think any of them had anything to do with it, do you?"

"I don't think anything yet," I said.

"What are you going to do now?"

"Make a couple of phone calls and go to bed. I can't start on any of this tonight."

"Mitch," she said, "I'm glad you're doing this."

"I know you are," I said, and went off to make my phone calls, two of them, to old friends on the force, men I could still think of as friends even with things as they are. I wanted to know if the investigating detectives had any reason other than theory to believe that Terry Wilford and Irene Boles had some connection prior to the murders. I asked my two friends to see if they could find out for me, both promised to try but gave no guarantee they could learn anything, and then I went to bed.

I couldn't get to sleep. I was thinking about the murders now, despite myself, and my head was full of short thin straight black lines, all disconnected. Sooner or later they would come together, like magnets, and form an arrow, and the arrow would point at a face, but for now they were only lines, each separate, some no doubt extraneous, each a stray name or stray fact. I lay looking at the ceiling, watching the lines float in my head.

The phone sounded a little before midnight. It was Hulmer.

"I'm at Vicki's," he said. "Donlon followed us. He's outside somewhere."

"Did he do anything besides follow you?"

"No."

"He's trying to scare you, keep you from making trouble."

"I'm staying here tonight," he said. "I don't want that weird cat bugging Vicki."

"Let me know if anything else happens," I said.

13

I HADN'T heard from Hulmer again, nor from either of my acquaintances on the force, by ten the next morning when I left the house and took the subway to Manhattan.

It was going to be another miserable day, hot and humid, the air heavy with sunlight and rancid moisture. When I stepped outside at ten o'clock the world already had the characteristic feel of hot wet wool, and one had the feeling of walking doggedly through some substance thicker than air. I wore a short-sleeved white shirt open at the throat, no tie, and by the time I'd walked to the subway stop the shirt was drenched and sticking to my skin.

The train I rode was nearly empty. The fans helped a little, but at the other end of the ride was Manhattan, which was even closer and muggier than Queens. Because there's no sensible subway method for getting to the Lower East Side, and because I've never been able to understand the Manhattan bus lines, I splurged and took a cab downtown. It turned out to be air-conditioned, the only time I'd ever been lucky enough to get one of those, though at first the luck didn't seem entirely good; my sopping shirt turned ice-cold, and I sat there shivering, thoughts of pneumonia circling in my head while people on the other side of the window glass were fanning themselves with magazines.

Just as I had gotten used to the cool dry air inside the cab we arrived at the new headquarters of the New World Samaritans. Another store front, the windows here were painted a flat white, plus a great deal of gold lettering. The window to the left of the entrance said, near the top, *New World Samaritans,* and below that, *American Cathedral.* Filling out the rest of the window were groups and clusters of words, among them *Have You Been Saved?, Bishop Walter Johnson Resident Custodian, All Welcome, Open Twenty-four hrs, Jesus Will Succor You, Enter and Make Your Peace with God,* and so on. The window on the other side, without repeating any of the phrasing, continued the same sentiments, while the white-painted glass of the door merely read *Entrance to Salvation.*

Leaving the cab was like walking into a closet full of overcoats. Almost nauseated, I hurried across the sidewalk and into the— store? church? cathedral? mission?

The inside was astonishing. I'd expected the usual grubby Lower East Side store front, plus some chairs or benches. Instead I'd walked into a cool dim pale room that made me think of California monasteries. The walls had been done over in rough plaster and painted white; there were dark wood beams across the otherwise white ceiling, the floor was good old wood dark with oil, and about a dozen rows of pews—dark wood, well polished—faced a muted dim altar at the far end of the room, the altar done in white with gold and purple trim. Some kind of ivy stretched across the wall behind the altar, looking cool and serene.

The air in here was cool, rather dry, very pleasant, much more natural than that inside the cab. As I walked down the central aisle toward the altar I felt my body relaxing, as though in some strange and unexpected way I'd turned a corner and there in front of me was home. I very nearly smiled, just to be there, and the feeling was in no way religious or mystical; it was, in fact, mostly architectural, the delight of these pale dim surroundings contrasting with the muckiness of the world outside.

There was no one in this room, but I found I was in no hurry to seek anyone out. I stood in front of the altar, looking at the few objects on its white-draped surface: candlesticks, a large open book, a brass goblet, a black square cloth edged in gold, and so on. Even seeing that the climbing ivy on the rear wall was artificial—it would, I suppose, have to be—didn't affect the grip the place had on me.

I don't know how long I stood there, but I didn't move until an unobtrusive door to the right of the altar opened and a man in a floor-length white robe with a white rope braid belt came through and said, "Good morning, brother." He shut the door behind himself and walked over to me, saying, "It was good of you to come to see us."

Everything was right about him but the face, which belonged not to a monk but to a bank clerk or post-office employee. It was round, pale, weak-featured, with pale blue eyes behind glasses with light plastic frames. But he was balding, with a very tonsure-like effect, and his voice was deep and confident and sympathetic.

I said, "I'd like to speak to Bishop Johnson."

"Ah," he said. "Then your purpose here is a secular one."

"I'm Mitchell Tobin. I believe Abraham Selkin phoned the bishop I'd be coming."

"Possibly," he said. "I'll go tell the bishop you're here."

"Thank you."

"Not at all." He turned away, went to the door, and paused there to look back at me again and say, "And yet, brother, when I first saw you I believe you had another purpose in your head."

I glanced at the altar, and looked back at him. "That may be," I said. "But it will have to wait."

"Salvation always has to wait," he said, and went through the doorway, and left me alone.

I looked at the altar again, frowning, asking myself: *What did he see in my face?* When he'd opened the door, for just a second or two I'd been unaware of his presence. What had been on my face then? What had I been thinking about, standing here in this pseudo-monastery?

My days on the force. An acrid nostalgia had crept into my mind, bringing me scenes from those days, tinged with brass-green as though the memories had been too long in a trunk in a galleon sunk at the bottom of the sea. I'd been remembering small moments of companionship with Jock Sheehan, who had been my partner, and small moments of pleasure with Linda Campbell, in whose bed I had been while Jock was being shot to death.

I wanted to talk to someone. I picked through a filing cabinet in my mind, turning over card after card, going through the names of all my friends, my former friends, my acquaintances, my relatives, everyone, looking for someone to whom I could go and say the million words I hadn't said in the last year.

I even wanted to talk to the tonsured white-robed bank clerk. But that would be self-indulgent, useless and away from the point. The point was the murder of Terry Wilford, the murder of Irene Boles, the probable murder of George Padbury, the arrest of Robin Kennely, the possible threat to either myself or the other partners in Thing East. Even if there were anything to be gained in making it possible for the million unsaid words to be said—and I didn't believe there was—this was neither the time nor the place for it.

I'm sure there was nothing in my face to intrigue the white-robed man when he returned. I was under control, standing near the door, going over in my mind the questions I intended to ask Bishop Johnson.

The white-robed man looked at me and nodded as though he'd just won a bet with himself. "The bishop will be happy to see you," he said. "If you'll come with me?"

I followed him into a small beige room with a few armchairs and end tables—clearly a place for talk—and on to a flight of stairs leading upward. We went up to the third floor and down a narrow dark gray corridor lined with doors and into an absolutely bare room furnished only with two white kitchen chairs facing each other in the middle of the floor. Two windows, heavy with dust but completely without drapes or curtains or shades or blinds or anything else, looked out over Avenue A and Tompkins Square Park. My guide said, "The bishop will be with you in a moment," and went out, shutting the door behind him.

The room was square, about ten feet on a side, with gray walls and a stained yellowing ceiling. Faded dark-patterned linoleum was on the floor. The paint on the two chairs was chipped. The upper pane of glass in the right-hand window was cracked, the crack covered with masking tape peeling loose at one end.

This was what one should expect from a building in this neighborhood, and the contrast with that first-floor chapel was unnerving. Why had they left this room like this? Why intensify its bleakness even more, with bare windows and less than the minimum of furniture?

I went over to one of the windows and looked out at the park, which was full of children, running and riding the swings and playing basketball as though there were no such thing as humidity. I stood and looked out the window and refused to let my mind drift from my purpose.

It was only two or three minutes before the door opened and Bishop Walter Johnson walked in, surprising me; I'd expected for some reason to be left alone here for a considerable time.

Bishop Johnson himself was also surprising. I hadn't been sure what to expect Bishop Johnson to be, but in my list of possibilities I wouldn't have included a slender handsome crew-cut thirty-year-old blind man in a dapper pale gray suit and pearl-gray tie.

He entered, shut the door, took two strides into the room, smiled at air, stuck his hand out, and said, "Mr. Tobin? I'm happy to know you. Abe called last night, told us you'd be coming along."

I hurried over from the window, not wanting his hand to be suspended alone in midair overlong. "How do you do? Bishop Johnson?"

"That's right." His smile was strong, self-confident, and so was his handshake. "Sit down," he said, and gestured toward one of the kitchen chairs, himself walking without hesitation to the other one and sitting down.

It was difficult to look at him. His blindness was of a kind that marred his eyes, leaving them flawed and wrinkled and gray, a shocking error in his handsome face. He must have realized this, because he was no sooner seated than he took out dark glasses and put them on. I understood that he had come into the room without them so I would know at once that he was blind, and I found myself admiring the unobtrusive control this man had on his environment.

Seated facing him, I said, "I suppose Selkin told you what I want to see you about."

"I think so. The murders, naturally. But mostly about keys."

"Yes. There's some question how Irene Boles—she's the girl who was murdered also."

"Yes, I know."

"Well. There's some question how she got into the building."

He nodded. "Naturally you want to know how many keys there are and who has them."

"Yes."

"There are two in this building," he said. "One with several other loose keys in an old Sucrets box in my middle desk drawer in my office upstairs. I've checked, and it's still there. The other one is on a large ring of keys always to be found in the pocket of Riggs, our resident janitor, and it too is still where it should be." He cocked his head to one side. "And now I suppose you want to know if there's any connection between Irene Boles and the New World Samaritans."

I did, but it surprised me he would guess that in advance. I said, "Is there any?"

He spread his hands. "Not that I've been able to discover. None of our residents knows any woman by that name, though of course some of them have had dealings at one time or another with women of her type. Of course I'll continue to inquire, and if anything does turn up I'll be happy to phone you and let you know."

"Thank you." It was all going very swiftly, he answering my questions even before I could ask them, volunteering cooperation before it was requested. I wasn't getting a chance to think about his answers, decide what I thought about him and them. I said, "But of course if one of your residents did have a connection with Irene Boles, he might be unlikely at this point to admit it."

Gently he said, "We don't lie to each other in this building, Mr. Tobin."

"Murderers lie wherever they are," I said. "Their lives are at stake."

"One's soul can also be at stake," he said. "And there is no murderer in this building, that I assure you. Your murderer is somewhere in the outside world, Mr. Tobin."

"Perhaps."

"When you learn more about us," he said, "you will know why I can speak with such assurance."

"You may be right," I said. "There is something else I want to talk to you about, though."

He smiled broadly. "I know," he said. "Why Thing East?"

"You're ahead of me again," I said, beginning to be irritated by him. "It does seem unlikely for a religious organization to rent space for a Greenwich Village coffee house."

"Unlikely? Why unlikely?"

"The image seems wrong," I said. "The young people who hang out in coffee houses tend to be not very religious."

"Still," he said, "a coffee house is hardly a den of iniquity. No black masses, no gambling, no prostitution, not even alcohol. There's no conflict between church and coffee, Mr. Tobin. The only conflict, really, is between the stereotypes in your own imagination."

"Of course," I said, a little irritated, "I don't know that much about your religion . . ."

"You don't?" His smile was frankly mocking now. "A religion with a name you've never heard of? In a store front? On the Lower East Side? Surely, Mr. Tobin, you *do* believe you know us."

"This place is different," I said, "I can see that. I do have an open mind, Bishop."

He put his head on one side again and sat there as though staring at me, the illusion increased by the dark glasses. Thoughtfully, perhaps to himself, he said, "Do I owe you an apology?"

"Not at all," I said, not understanding him.

"Brother William," he said, "told me he thought you were troubled by something unconnected with your stated purpose here. He has very good eyes, you know. I only wish my ears were as perceptive. I've heard only truculence in your voice, and I mistook it for the contempt of the shallow mind, a reaction I have grown used to. But Brother William was right, wasn't he? What I've been hearing is your struggle not to talk about what's really on your mind."

"If so," I said, "I intend to win the struggle. Had you known Terry Wilford before he came to you to rent your old place?"

He hesitated, as though wanting to pursue the other subject, but then said, "No, that was our first meeting. Mrs. Joyce Regan brought him, he was a friend of her son Edwin."

"Did you agree to the idea of a coffee house right away?"

"No, I didn't. We hadn't planned to rent the store area at all; in fact, we've been looking for someone to buy the property. But Terry was quite insistent, and he did agree to vacate at once if we found someone interested in buying, so at last I said yes." He smiled in reminiscence. "Terry was quite a personality, friendly but very self-assured. And infectiously enthusiastic."

"You got caught up in his enthusiasm?"

"Yes, I did. Not that I ever expected them to make a long-range financial success there, but I thought they probably would enjoy themselves a great deal while it lasted."

"What was the rent?"

"We settled on eighty dollars a month," he said.

That was low for that part of the city, maybe half the rental Bishop Johnson could legitimately have asked. I said, "How long had the place been empty?"

"We moved here in February."

"Six months ago?"

"You seem surprised."

"The chapel on the first floor looks—older."

"Some of our residents are quite clever at do-it-yourself projects," he said.

I said, "On the window downstairs it says 'American Cathedral.' Are there others?"

He smiled again, saying, "No, I'm afraid not. Some of our residents are also quite optimistic about our future. I haven't seen the windows myself, of course, but I understand the brothers who did them were—enthusiastic." He laughed, adding, "Infectiously enthusiastic, like Terry Wilford."

"Someone didn't catch the infection," I said, and got to my feet. "I want to thank you for your time—"

"Not at all," he said, rising. "I don't know if I've helped you at all on your quest."

"I don't know myself yet," I said.

"On the other thing," he said, smiling gently at me, "perhaps we *could* help you."

"It isn't necessary," I said. "Thank you, but I can handle it myself."

"I'm sure you can. Still, if you should ever want to talk I'll be more than happy to listen."

I didn't like the offer, it was presumptuous and somehow insulting. He had no right to think he knew me that easily. Stiffly I said, "I'll remember that. Thank you."

"Of course. If you'll just wait a moment, I'll have Brother William escort you back downstairs."

He started for the door, but I said, "That won't be necessary. I can find my way."

"We'd prefer it if you had an escort," he said blandly, and turned with his hand on the knob. "Don't worry, Mr. Tobin. He won't pry."

"All right," I said, and turned my back on him, which of course he couldn't see. He went out, closing the door after him, and I went over to the window and looked out again at the park.

As I watched, Donlon got up from the bench he'd been sitting on, near the sidewalk at this end of the park, and walked over to his black unmarked Ford. He reached in, got a pack of cigarettes from the glove compartment, and strolled back to his bench, opening the package and tossing the cellophane and foil away. Children ran around him like foaming wavelets around a rock. He didn't look over at this building at all.

When Brother William came in, I said, "Is there a back way out?"

"Has to be, brother," he said. "That's why we're not at the old place any more."

"That's the way I want to go," I said.

"Might I ask why?"

I motioned at the window. "There's a policeman out there, he's been following me. I want to get away from him."

Brother William came over to the window. "Where is he?"

"Sitting on the bench there by the—"

"Donlon!"

I looked at Brother William in surprise. "You know him?"

"The sweetest thing about moving over here," he said, "is that we got at last out of Detective Donlon's territory." He looked at me. "And now have you brought him back to us?"

"What was the problem with him? At the old place?"

Brother William stood gazing out the window. "A troubled man," he said. "He must find filth. Find it or make it."

"What did he do?"

"Searched for filth," he said. He shook his head and added, "No one could ever reach him. He didn't want to be reached." He turned away, saying, "Come along, I'll show you the rear way out."

On the way down I tried to get him to be more explicit about what Donlon had done, but all I got was more of the same. From the sound of it, Donlon had been working the same tactics with the church as he'd tried later with the coffee house; steady minor harassment, constant irritating visits, a frustrating lack of definiteness of purpose.

The rear door led onto a garbage-strewn alley leading leftward to East Ninth Street. Brother William pointed the way I should go and then said, "Good luck, brother."

Good luck. With Donlon? With the search for the murderer of Terry Wilford? With the unstated other problem? Brother William closed the door before I could ask.

14

THE APARTMENT was on the fourth floor of a walk-up, in which the stairwell mugginess was complemented by the brackish stink of old urine. I paused in front of the door to catch my breath before knocking. My shirt was sopping again and I was starting a dull headache.

I knocked, and waited quite a long while, and the door was at last opened an inch by a girl who showed me nothing but one sliver of her face, dominated by a large brown eye. She blinked at me and said, "Yes?"

It was after eleven by now, but there was only darkness in the apartment behind her. I said, "Did I wake you? I'm sorry, I'll come back later."

"No, that's okay, we have to get up anyway. What did you want?"

"You're Ann?"

Puzzled, she said, "That's right. So?"

"And Jack Parker is here?"

"It's his place. What do you want?"

"My name is Mitchell Tobin," I said. "I'm Robin Kennely's cousin."

"Robin— Oh! Terry's girl." Her face and voice had hardened. "We know about *her*," she said.

"What do you know about her?"

"It doesn't matter. You're her cousin?"

"Second cousin," I said, knowing the age difference was what was bothering her. "I'd like to speak to Jack, if he's around."

"Well, I guess so," she said. She seemed at a loss, the one visible eye blinking and looking all around. "Uhhhh," she said, "hold on a second." And shut the door.

I waited, two or three minutes, and then the door opened the same inch again, showing the same vertical sliver of face, and she said, "What do you want to talk to him about?"

"I'm trying to help Robin," I said. "I want to talk to him about the people who knew Terry."

"What about them?"

"Who they are, if any of them might have known the girl who was killed, any ideas he might have about who did the killings, things like that."

"It said in the paper Robin did it."

"That's why I'm trying to help her. I don't believe the paper."

She considered, the eye studying me thoughtfully, and then abruptly she said, "Hold on a second," again, and once more shut the door.

This time the wait was longer, and I'd just about decided to start knocking on the door when it opened exactly as before, and she said, "Jack says he doesn't know anything, he can't help you. Sorry."

She would have shut the door then, but quickly I said, "Then I'll talk to you."

The eye gazed at me, unblinking. "Why me?" she said in a flat tone.

"You knew Terry, too," I reminded her. "You used to go with him."

"That was a long time ago."

"Six months. Still, you know the people he knew, the places he went to, the kind of trouble he might have made for himself."

"You know an awful lot, don't you?" she said, much more wary now.

"Not very much, yet," I said. "I need to know a lot more."

"Then talk to the cops."

"They can't help me."

"Neither can we," she said, and shut the door.

Knock on it? Force the issue? No, I had no authority vested in me these days, I could only try for cooperation. And though I could understand why these two people were wary of me, wary of any connection being made between them and the death of Terry Wilford, I did want their cooperation. I'd have to try a more roundabout method.

I went back out to the frying-pan street and down to the corner, where there was a drugstore without air-conditioning. In a phone booth in which the fan didn't work I took out my notebook and first tried Hulmer Fass's number, and when he proved not to be home, I called Abe Selkin instead.

Selkin answered on the first ring. I identified myself and said, "I just tried to talk to Jack Parker. He wouldn't see me. Do you know him well enough to convince him I'm all right?"

"I'm sorry, Mr. Tobin, no can do. Jack and I just know each other to talk to, we've never been buddies."

"Do you know anyone else who could do it?"

"Get him to talk to you? Let me think a second."

"Certainly."

The phone hummed in my ear, and at last he said, "There's one guy. He's a maybe. Let me try him and call you back."

"You can't. I'll call you in—how long? Half an hour?"

"Make it an hour. I might have trouble finding the guy."

"An hour." I looked at my watch. "Just around noon," I said. "Fine."

I left the phone booth and the air outside seemed almost cool for a minute. In the Manhattan phone book on the rack beside the booth I found the name Bodkin, Claude 87 W 63. It was a better address than I'd expected for a man described to me as a mooch, but there were unlikely to be two Claude Bodkins in New York, so I went back into the airless phone booth and called him. I got a recording machine which advised me, in Bodkin's somewhat nasal voice, that he was not at home and I had thirty seconds in which to leave my message. I hung up without speaking.

I walked back up First Avenue to East Eleventh Street—it seemed endless under that sun—and right to Ed Regan's address, he being the friend of Terry Wilford's whose mother was a New World Samaritan. Wilford himself had lived in this building—an ordinary brick tenement with tan peeling hallways—until moving illegally into the Thing East building.

I went inside, to the same smell of stale urine as in Jack Parker's building on Houston Street, and near the foot of the stairs I saw two giggling olive-skinned barely dressed young boys scratching words into the wall with a jagged piece of broken Coke bottle. One of them looked at me and, grinning, said something in Spanish. "In your hat," I said amiably, and went on up the stairs.

The mailbox in the foyer had given Regan's apartment number as ten, which I found on the third floor. I knocked, and after a minute the door was opened by a disheveled young man covered with varicolored paint. His hair was shaggy and uncombed, he wore eyeglasses with patched tortoise-shell frames, his T-shirt and baggy brown trousers were spattered with paint, and on his feet were tattered white sneakers. To complete the picture, he held upright in his right hand an artist's brush tipped with gleaming wet red.

"How do you do?" I said, feeling oddly like a door-to-door salesman. "My name is Mitchell Tobin. I believe Abe Selkin phoned you about—"

"Oh, right! Come in, come in."

There seemed to be a great urgency in what he said, so I stepped right in and he briskly shut the door behind me, saying, "I didn't know when you'd be here exactly, so I just went ahead and went to work."

"If you'd rather I came back later I could—"

"No, no! It's perfectly all right, I can work while we talk." He smiled proudly. "I'm doing a portrait of my mother."

I felt I was supposed to say something approving, so I said, "That's good."

"Well," he said, pleased but trying for modesty, "we'll see how it works out. Come on along."

I had entered into the kitchen, which was much cleaner than the general run of kitchens in this neighborhood but otherwise standard. Thick layers of paint covered every surface, the stove and refrigerator were ancient relics, the doors didn't quite close on the wall cabinets, and under the high narrow window was an old bathtub on legs, covered with an oilskin-lined board, on which stood gradated white canisters with red tops and red lettering reading COFFEE TEA SUGAR FLOUR.

A narrow windowless hallway led down from this kitchen, and through it I followed Ed Regan. Several paintings hung on both walls, but it was too dim to really make them out, except that they all seemed to be portraits of the same woman: stocky, gray-haired, in dark clothing, seated.

The original was in the living room, sitting on a wooden kitchen chair in the light from two tall windows, in which the panes sparkled with cleanliness. An easel stood in the middle of the room, a curved palette lay amid squeezed tubes of paint on a table to one side of the easel, and in front of the easel was a tall black stool. A large piece of paint-spattered gray canvas covered the floor in the area of the easel, and the rest of the floor was bare wood, polished to a high gloss. A maroon sofa with doilies on the arms was along the opposite wall, a television set stood on a wheeled stand in a corner, and around the perimeter of the room were the ordinary tables and chairs and lamps.

Ed Regan said, "Mother, this is the man Abe Selkin told me

about." And then, more formally, "Mother, Mr. Mitchell Tobin. Mr. Tobin, my mother, Victorina Regan."

We both said how-do-you-do and she invited me to sit down on the sofa. She was a woman in her late fifties, medium height, stocky, pleasant-faced, matronly, maternal. Her dress was plain, her stockings dark, her shoes sensible. She had done her own hair, probably in the same style for the last fifteen years.

I sat down where she had suggested, where I could see both her and the painting her son was working on. It was a bit idealized, but was otherwise a realistic portrayal of the woman, the chair, the window, the wall. Ed Regan put a dab of red on a section of the window, reached for his stool, and apparently became at once lost in his work. His mother, her head held stiffly, looked at me catty-corner and said, "I understand you're related to the Kennely girl."

"Second cousin."

"A nice enough girl. Rather young, of course. Though we can't hold youth against a person, can we?"

"I suppose not," I said.

"Still," she said, "some people do seem to insist on staying young entirely too long for their own good. The Wilford boy, for one. He would have been a bad influence on Edwin if we'd let him."

"Oh, Terry never meant any harm," the son said, jollying his mother, and turned briefly to flash me a smile glazed with embarrassment.

"I'm sure not," his mother said. "Youth never means any harm, that's one of its characteristics. But youth is waste, Edwin. Waste of time, waste of resources, waste of God's precious talents. If more young men were like you, how much better a world this would be."

"Everyone has to pick his own path, Mother."

"Naturally. I only thank God you've chosen the path of wisdom."

I felt I was present for a conversation which had been repeating itself, with variants, for years, and I preferred something more topical, so I said, "Mrs. Regan, did you discourage Terry Wilford from seeing your son?"

"Not at all," she said, affecting surprise. "Edwin is a free agent. He and young Wilford saw a great deal of each other for a period of time. Until Wilford became involved in the restaurant and moved across town."

"Restaurant? Oh, you mean Thing East."

"Yes, the place where he was murdered."

"I understand you had something to do with getting that location for him."

"I did introduce him to the bishop, yes."

"So he said. I spoke to him a little while ago."

"Bishop Johnson?"

"Yes. A remarkable man."

"A saint, Mr. Tobin. I don't know what religion you are . . ."

She let the sentence hang there for me to finish, but I chose not to, saying instead, "Yes, I was very impressed by him. He told me you brought Terry Wilford to see him, and now I'm wondering, if you disapproved of him, why you helped him that way."

"I didn't disapprove of him, Mr. Tobin," she said, somewhat stiffly. "I don't disapprove of anyone, I believe every one of us has the right to choose his or her own road. I would prefer not to have anyone I cared deeply for tarry long on the road where young Wilford seemed inclined to stay, but I would hardly condemn anyone who decided *that* was where he wanted to be."

"I see."

"And of course I was delighted," she went on, "when he took an interest in starting something substantial. He had great energy and great imagination, and I was delighted at the chance to help him begin to put his talents to use."

"Of course," I said, beginning to understand the rules this woman lived by. From the look of the apartment, she lived here, with her son, which had to be an unusual situation; a boy goes off to the East Village to live in a tenement and be a painter, and his mother goes along with him. It would take a remarkable woman to bring that off, and it seemed as though she had done it.

Of course, the son in such a situation would tend to fade into his mother's shadow if he weren't a strong and sturdy personality himself, which Ed Regan wasn't. Wanting to try to comprehend the boy somewhat, I turned to him now, apparently absorbed in his painting, and said, "Ed, you know most of the people in Terry's crowd. Would you say he had many enemies?"

"Enemies?" He paused, his brush this time tipped with pearl-gray, and stood gazing at a corner of the ceiling. Frowning, he said, "Somebody who'd want to kill him, you mean?"

"Not necessarily. Just anyone who might have a grudge against him or dislike him for any reason."

"Huh." He shrugged, and frowned now at the painting, and said, "Well, there's Jack Parker. I suppose you could call him an enemy of Terry's." He looked at me. "Not that he'd want to kill Terry or anything like that," he said. "But Jack doesn't like Terry. Didn't like him."

"With perfectly adequate cause," Mrs. Regan added. "Youth again, fickle, flitting back and forth, never knowing its own mind."

I said to the son, "I've already heard about Jack Parker. Anybody else?"

He touched the gray to the canvas, frowned at the result, frowned at his palette, finally shook his head. "Nobody," he said. "Terry was an easygoing guy, he got along with just about everybody. Even Mother," he added, and grinned at me.

The mother smiled, too, indulgently, and said, "I'm just everyone's den mother, Mr. Tobin. You know how it is."

I knew how she wanted it to be, though I had no way of knowing whether or not that was the way it actually was. Nor could I think of anything else to ask either of them. They were both deeply involved in some half-fantasy life plan of their own, and I doubted if any third party ever made much of an impression on them.

On a sudden impulse, I asked Ed Regan, "Do you know Vicki Oppenheim?"

I'd expected the mother to answer, and she did. "Now *there's* a one! Think what that girl could be if she wanted, and how she wastes herself. *There's* someone who should talk to Bishop Johnson."

"Any day now," Ed Regan told me, grinning, "Mother's going to promote Bishop Johnson to God."

"Saint is high enough," his mother said. "You remember what he told *you,* young man."

I got to my feet, saying, "Well, thank you for your time. I appreciate it."

"Anything we can do," the son said. "We both like Robin, don't we, Mother?"

"Of course. A really sweet young thing. Frankly, Mr. Tobin, I believe you have right on your side. That young girl *couldn't* have murdered anybody that way."

"That's what I think, too," I said, and moved toward the door. "Thank you again. No, that's all right," I told the son, as he started away from the easel, "I can find my own way out, you keep on with your work. It's coming along very well."

"You think so?" He smiled fondly at the painting.

I went back down the dim hall and out of the apartment and down the stairs. At the foot of the stairs on the first floor the two boys were still scratching away with the Coke bottle shard, patiently and gigglingly printing out some long involved and no doubt scatological paragraph in Spanish. They looked up at me as I started down the last flight, and their faces changed, their attention diverted to something above me.

I looked up, and something black was hurtling down the center of the stairwell. These first-floor stairs were wider than the ones above, I'd been holding the banister, I was directly beneath.

I leaped to the side, lost my footing on the slate stair, fell heavily, heard something crash and boom behind my head, and a second later there was a scream that choked off in midstride. I slid painfully down several steps, thumping my sides and back, before I finally managed to stop myself and sit up and look around.

At the foot of the stairs one of the two boys was standing ashen-faced against the wall. The other one was lying on his back at the foot of the stairs with a large square black metal box sitting canted on his head and shoulders. Maroon liquid trickled across the floor from under the box.

The living boy began to vomit.

15

AN APARTMENT on the first-floor front was taken over by the police, and it was there a heavy red-faced bored uniformed sergeant interrogated me. "I went up the stairs to the roof," I told him, "but of course by the time I got up there he was gone. The roof door was open. I went out there and didn't see anybody at all."

The sergeant didn't really care what had happened. A black iron chimney cap, eighteen inches square, six inches high, slightly peaked at the top, weight about thirty pounds, which had been lying unused on the roof near the chimney recently replaced, had been dropped down the stairwell by party or parties unknown, maybe for fun, maybe for serious, and had killed a spic kid, maybe on purpose, maybe by accident. There were unanswered questions, but slums are built of unanswered questions, and the sergeant obviously had little expectation of ever finding the answers to this group of them. He laboriously took down in his notebook what I said to him, took my name and address, told me I might be called for the inquest, and I was free to go. I went through the mob of people still clustered in the hallway, through the second mob outside on the sidewalk, and away.

I hadn't told the sergeant any more than the bare facts of the event. He hadn't asked me what I was doing in that building, and I hadn't volunteered the information. Therefore he had no way of knowing that the death of the child might be connected with three other recent deaths, nor would it have done him any good if I had told him, since the police believed they already had the murderess in custody on two of the deaths, and the third had not been listed as a homicide.

It was possible that someone on the force working on the Wilford killing might stumble across my name in a report in connection with the child's death and might follow it up out of curiosity and therefore learn that the address of the incident was Terry Wilford's former address, and so ultimately come knocking at my door to find out what I was doing and why, and of course at that point I would have to be detailed and truthful—mostly—in my answers. But the possibility was a slender one, given the size of the force, the fact that the child's death had occurred in a different precinct, and the fact that the Wilford and Boles deaths were no longer active police concerns but had been turned over by now for further action to the district attorney's office. In any event, I had at the very least bought myself additional time.

The child had bought me some time, too. If he hadn't looked up, if he hadn't drawn my attention to the black shape plummeting downward, he would have been the witness sitting in front of the bored sergeant and I would have been the body at the foot of the stairs.

It had been meant for me, that much was obvious. The murderer was unsure of himself, worried, afraid his traces weren't adequately hidden. That was why he'd killed George Padbury, who had known something and been concealing it and had wanted to tell it to me on the phone half an hour before his death. And now the murderer was afraid of me, moving around, poking into this and that, stirring things up that were supposed to be neatly under control. And when he was afraid, this murderer, he killed again.

Was he around me now, watching from somewhere? Had he

stayed in the neighborhood to see if things had gone well, and did he now know he would have to try again? It was more likely he'd gone far away, gone to ground for a while, whether or not he knew he'd missed me.

So I probably had some free time, free from police and murderer both. I'd do with it as much as I could.

There was a candy store on the corner, full of children drinking soda. I threaded through them to the phone booth and called Abe Selkin.

He said, "Jack doesn't want any part of you, Mr. Tobin. He knows you used to be a cop, he knows you're related to Robin, he thinks you're out to frame him to get her off the hook."

"That's not very sensible," I said.

"I know it. But that's what he thinks."

"All right. Thanks, anyway. Is there anybody at Thing East now?"

"Sure. Hully's over there, maybe Vicki. We're open again, the cops let us open yesterday."

"Good."

"Let me know if there's anything I can do."

"I will."

I hung up and tried Claude Bodkin's number again, and this time he was home. And out of breath. "Just a second," he said. "I'm winded."

I waited, listening to heavy breathing, until finally he said, "All right. Sorry about that, I was doing my exercises." His voice was somewhat more nasal than it had been on his machine.

I said, "My name is Mitchell Tobin, Mr. Bodkin. I don't know if you read in the paper about Terry Wilford being murdered?"

"God, yes. Talk about melodrama."

"The young lady who's been arrested," I said, "Robin Kennely, is my cousin. We're trying to work up a defense for her, so naturally we want to talk to anybody who knew the Wilford boy. I understand you used to be his roommate?"

"God, that was years ago."

"A year and a half, as I understand it."

"Is that all? God, time flies. To tell you the truth, Mr.—what did you say your name was?"

"Tobin, Mitchell Tobin."

"Well, to tell you the truth, Mitch—may I call you Mitch?"

"Go right ahead," I said. So long as I could ask him my questions, he could call me any name he liked.

"To tell you the truth, Mitch," he said, starting the same sentence for the third time, "I hardly know Robin Kennely at all, and I haven't seen Terry since we stopped rooming together. I mean, I doubt I could give you anything *current,* you see what I mean?"

"It's not current facts we're looking for," I said. "It's mostly Terry's personality, his character, that I want to know about. Any incidents you might know of that would help to show the kind of person he was."

"Oh, God, if *that's* what you want I could talk a week. Listen, where are you now?"

"Downtown."

"Well, I have a thing at five, and then the evening's shot, of course. We could have a drink now, if you like. How about the Newfoundland Donkey?"

"I don't believe I know it."

"Lex and Sixty-first, you can't miss it. Shall we say one?"

"One, that's fine."

"The question is," he said, "how are we going to recognize one another? Wait, I know. I'll wear my lemon-lime shirt. It's short sleeves, yellow and green vertical stripes. I doubt there'll be more than one such shirt in the Donkey in the middle of the day."

"Fine."

"And I'll be sitting at the bar, down toward the end."

"All right. See you at one."

"Ta."

It was now barely twelve, so I walked back down to Houston Street to try a frontal attack on Jack Parker, but there was no answer to my knock. Either they had prepared themselves for a siege or they'd gone out.

There was a large delicatessen a block away. I had lunch there, walked back through the midday heat to try Parker once more, got no answer again, and took a cab uptown.

It was not air-conditioned. I felt cheated.

16 ———————————

THE Newfoundland Donkey was obviously what the magazines would call an In bar. It seemed arch and pretentious to me, but the lighting was dim enough and the wood dark enough so that the décor could readily be ignored. The air-conditioning was on full blast, and I was chilled to the bone by the time I sat down at the bar. When the bartender asked me what I wanted I was tempted to ask for a hot toddy, but settled on beer instead.

There was no one here with a lemon-lime shirt on, but it was only five till one, so I settled down with my beer—bottled, no draft—and looked at the other customers.

They were mostly men, young to middle-aged, slender, well dressed, chatting animatedly with one another, bright young executives drinking their lunches. Beyond the bar was a restaurant area, deep and narrow and dark, lit mostly by the candles in red glass at each table, and a few women were spotted at the tables back there: sleek and efficient-looking and stylish rather than pretty.

I finished my first beer at five after one and my second at one-fifteen. I decided to nurse the third one till one-thirty, and if he hadn't arrived by then I'd phone him. In the meantime men kept coming into the place, the door opening with flashes of that bristling bright sunlight outside, but none of them was dressed right to be Bodkin. I drank my third beer a sip at a time, I watched the customers, I watched the moving and flashing and bobbing beer and whiskey ads on the back bar, I watched my watch.

He came in at one twenty-eight, a short slender childish-looking young man in the threatened shirt, pale chinos, scuffed white sneakers, flaming red hair, and the darkest sunglasses I've ever seen. I motioned to him and he came over, smiling and waving his hands and talking long before he was close enough for me to hear.

". . . how it is," he said, and slid into the stool next to mine. "You get on the damn horn, they won't let you off. Since I got into communications I practically sleep with that damn phone to my ear. Beefeater and Schweppes, Jerry. What's that you're drinking, beer? God. You go out in that heat, you'll sweat buckets. Let's grab a table. Jerry, we'll be over there."

I followed him to a table on the opposite wall. We sat down and he said, "I've been thinking about Terry, Mitch, and I really don't know what I can tell you. Terry and I didn't hit it off, that's true enough, but that could just be a personality thing, two people don't jell, you know what I mean? Ahh," he said, as his drink arrived, "that's what I've been wanting." He picked up the drink and said to me, "I've made a rule. Not a drop before one o'clock, no matter what. It's my pattern for success. Pip pip."

He took a healthy swallow, put the glass down, and said, "You know what they say, don't say anything against the dead. So what can I say? We had tiffs, everybody has tiffs, we didn't get along. You want a lot of roommate grievances, that's not going to do you any good. Terry and I knew each other vaguely from college, he was two years behind me, I was looking for a roommate, he was fresh in town and looked me up, we found a place, we didn't hit it off, I moved out, end of story."

I said, as he took another swallow of his drink, "I'd thought maybe you moved because your income went up."

"What, these threads?" He grinned, holding his arms out for

me to look at his clothing. "You like them? Custom sneakers, nothing but the best. But seriously, no, that isn't what happened. Affluence hit me two or three months later, when I made the break into communications." He finished his drink, held the empty glass over his head, and wig-wagged it at the barman.

I said, "I understand you and Wilford had a fight one time. I mean, physically, punching each other."

He put the glass down, grinned at me, and shook his head. "Not exactly," he said. "God, when I think of that. Look at me, Mitch, I'm no pugilist. Crippled newsies roll me for my shoes. Terry wiped up the floor with me, pure and simple, it was as easy as that."

I couldn't see his eyes through the gray-black lenses of his glasses, but the rest of his face showed only honest amusement. I said, "You don't seem to have held a grudge for it."

"Be pointless now, wouldn't it?" he said, and grinned again, shrugging his shoulders. "The poor bastard's dead. Besides, he was right. I'd racked up his car for him. I'd have done the same thing myself if I was some sort of Neanderthal."

"Is that what Terry was?"

"Ah hah!" he said happily, and pointed a finger at me. "You see? There *is* still hostility there! My analyst said there was, but I said no no no, it's all over, it's in the past and doesn't matter any more. Never disagree with your analyst, Mitch, they know things that are closed to ordinary men. Bless you, darling." This last to the waitress, who had brought his fresh drink.

As he took a first swallow of it I said, "As I understand it, you felt very strongly about it at the time. Tried to have Wilford arrested, didn't you?"

"God, yes. Talk about idiocy. He simply turned the fuzz right back at me, got me thirty days at Newgate. Because of that car of his." He had some more Beefeater and Schweppes. "My analyst tells me I'm glad Terry's dead. Do you suppose he's right?"

"I really don't know," I said. "Can you think of anybody else who might be glad he's dead?"

"God, no. Terry was one of your easy assimilators, everybody loved him. Hello there, Terry! Good old Terry! Long time no see, Terry! Made out with the women like a bandit. That was another thing. God, when I think how many rotten science-fiction movies I saw on Forty-second Street. We had a system, when the chain lock was on, it meant there was a girl in the place, the other guy had to go away for a while. Terry *always* had that damn chain up. You know how often I did?" He waited till I shook my head, then held up one triumphant finger, saying, "Once! And that was a damned fluke. A damned poor fluke, too, if you want to know."

He pulled again at his drink, said, "Of course, all that's changed now. You know how it is, some people blossom no matter what, but some need success, money, some sort of external symbol of value to build their self-esteem. That was me, all right. Once I got into communications, began to pull in the bread, it was a brand-new Claude. Two years ago, Mitch, I wouldn't have walked into a place like this in threads like these for all the tea in Berkeley. Now look at me."

"Success does make a difference," I agreed. I assumed it did, because I knew very well that failure did.

He looked at his watch. "She's always late," he said. "I hope you don't mind, Mitch, I'm doubling up, got a young lady meeting me here. Supposed to be here at one-thirty. Late, naturally."

I said, "Of course, you know I'm coming around because we don't think Robin killed Wilford."

"I figured that," he said. "Still, you know the old saying, hell hath no fury, and so on." He drained his glass, made his wig-wag signal to the barman again.

"We don't think Robin was a woman scorned," I said.

He looked at me blankly. "What say?"

"What you said. Hell hath no fury like a woman scorned. We don't think that's the way it happened."

"Well, sure. You wouldn't, naturally. But who knows, you could be right. I only met the girl two, three times, but she didn't strike me as the violent type. You know what I mean? Very mousy little girl."

"If Robin didn't kill him," I said, "somebody else must have."

"A is not B," he said, and nodded. "That's logic." Then, as his fresh drink arrived, "Thanks, sweets."

I said, "Can you think of anyone who might want to kill Terry Wilford?"

"A year and a half ago," he said, lifting his glass, "*I* wanted to. That's the only one I know. Mud in your eye."

As he drank I said, "What about Irene Boles?"

He finished swallowing, frowned, said, "Who?"

"The girl who was killed with him."

"Oh, the hooker! God, wasn't that a touch? Pure Dostoevski."

"Did you know her?"

"Who, me? No, she must have been new on the scene. Linda, love!"

This last was shouted past me. I turned and saw a startlingly beautiful blond young woman coming through the tables toward us. She carried a straw purse that kept bumping into people, she was dressed violently in pink, and she too was talking a mile a minute even though she was too far away to be heard.

She arrived at the table saying, ". . . how they are. Just beastly, love bun. I could have been there another two *hours* if I hadn't put my foot down. Hel-lo, sweetie."

She dipped for a kiss on the cheek and turned sea-blue eyes on me as Bodkin said, "Linda, Mitch. We've been engaged in melo-drama."

"How do you do," I said.

"Frazzled," she said, settling into the chair to my right. To Bodkin she said, "Get me a drink, love, before all my seams come undone."

"No sooner said," Bodkin told her, and began waving his arms vigorously at the bartender.

I said, "I'll put in the order for you on my way out."

His arms still in midair, as though I was holding him up, Bodkin looked at me and said, "We're done?"

"Unless you can think of something else, yes."

He lowered his arms. "Not a thing," he said. "I haven't seen any of those people in a lifetime, Mitch. God, when I think who I was then." He reached out and squeezed the girl's hand, saying to her, "You couldn't possibly believe it, darling."

I said, "What's the lady drinking?"

She answered for herself: "Beefeater and Schweppes. And thank you so much."

"Not at all. Nice to have met you."

I got to my feet, and Bodkin said, "Don't worry about that beer of yours, Mitch, it's on my tab."

I doubted he had a tab, since credit in bars is illegal in New York, but I let him have the gesture, which I knew he was making for the sake of the girl. I thanked him for both the beer and his time, went over to the bar to order the drink, and went outside to a world that now seemed twice as hot and twice as humid and twice as stuffy as before.

I hailed a cab—not air-conditioned—and on the way downtown I thought about Bodkin and decided he could not have had anything to do with the murders. Whatever frustration or hatred he had once felt for Terry Wilford was well under control by now. It was obviously true that he was carving out some sort of successful career for himself, and that success had changed him drastically from the mooch who had lived with Wilford.

I wondered what he did for a living. In all the times he'd mentioned his being "in communications," he hadn't managed once to communicate to me what his job was, or even what specific area he worked in. Was he in advertising? In television? Publishing? Public relations? Bell Telephone? Or did it no longer matter, did they all blend into one another after a while, so that the bright young men coming along these days were merely "in communications"?

The world is not one world, but a hundred thousand worlds,

overlapping and yet almost entirely sealed off from one another. Their perimeters are age or occupation or home address or any one of half a dozen other factors. I was someone who had been thrust out of his world to exist in limbo, and now in the search for Terry Wilford's murderer I was peeking and poking into worlds foreign to me, trying to understand their customs and languages, wondering where in these alien landscapes I would find the one with the blood-red hands.

Never in my life was I more conscious of these separate foreign worlds than in the twenty-five-minute cab ride from the Newfoundland Donkey to Thing East.

17

I EXPERIENCED a strong sensation of *déjà vu* upon entering Thing East, and for just a second I felt as though I'd been given another chance; George Padbury would be up front, Robin and Terry would be upstairs, and all I had to do was turn around at once, leave, take the subway back to Queens, and none of this would have happened.

The appearance of the place helped compound this irrational feeling. The same bright heat outside, the same dim coolness inside, the same first impression of emptiness, and the same sudden movement from the far right corner of the room.

Except that this time it was Hulmer, coming out of the kitchen. He saw me and called, "Mr. Tobin! Come on back."

I walked down amid the tables to him. "Hello, Hulmer. I came to see the upstairs."

"Abe called, said you'd be coming by."

We stepped through into the kitchen and Vicki was there, stacking clean plates. We exchanged hellos, and Hulmer said, "You want me to come up with you? Show you where everything was."

"I'd appreciate it."

Vicki said, "Want some iced tea? Just made fresh."

"Thank you, yes. With lemon, if you have it."

"Sure thing." Handing me the glass, she said, "The heat's terrible today, isn't it?"

"It's not so bad in here."

Hulmer said, "Wait till you get upstairs."

I could feel what he meant the minute he opened the door; a wave of hot dry attic-like heat poured out, enveloping us.

Hulmer led the way, saying over his shoulder, "Better watch your step, there isn't much light."

No, there wasn't. I followed him up the stairs—narrow, with gray walls on both sides—into dark gloomy heat. The perspiration that Claude Bodkin had warned me about poured from me.

At the head of the stairs the darkness was almost complete. Hulmer bent and lit a small shadeless table lamp sitting on the floor against the right-hand wall. "There isn't any electricity on up here," he explained. "Terry ran extension cords up from downstairs."

We were in a corridor running the length of the building, with boarded-up windows at both ends. Thin slivers of sunlight could be seen between the boards. With the lamp on, I could see the extension cords coming up the edge of the stairs and trailing away along the corridor.

For some reason I'd expected to find rubble up here, peeling plaster and scruffy stacks of old newspaper, but it wasn't like that at all. It was merely an empty building, under a layer of gray dust. The corridor was lined with wooden doors, all shut.

"Terry used the rooms along the right side," Hulmer told me. "Over this way."

He pushed open the first door on the right, and clear sunlight gleamed ahead of us. The room we entered was a long rectangle, with two windows at the end to our right. These had been boarded up, but the boards had been knocked loose, some entirely gone now and the others canted to the side, so that the early afternoon sun, still high in the sky, angled its light in to bounce off the wood floor and flood the room with a golden radiance. There was less dust in here, but the room didn't so much give an impression of having been lived in as of having been camped in.

The first thing I noticed was the walls, or that is to say the objects hung on the walls. Directly opposite the doorway was a large square abstract painting of the Jackson Pollock dribble school, done in various shades of dark blue-gray, with a streak of orange in the lower left corner. To the right of this was a *Times Magazine* cover showing student rioters at a sit-in at a western university. Beyond that was a large board covered with a montage of newspaper headlines, followed by a literal painting of a stop sign. In the opposite direction from the central blue-gray painting were a pair of crossed swords, a charcoal sketch of a girl who might have been Robin, and a huge photo of W. C. Fields.

The other walls were covered in much the same varied way, so that the total effect was of being in some avant-garde movie-house lobby after a bombing. I say after a bombing because of the furniture, or lack of furniture, which completed the place. There were two kitchen chairs to the right, a small bookcase containing phonograph components and a few magazines to the left, and a small round table draped with sweaters and slacks across the way.

Hulmer pointed to a conspicuously empty area in the far right corner and said, "That's where the bed was."

"Where the bodies were found?"

"Right. It wasn't really a bed, Terry didn't have nothing but a double-bed mattress. The cops took it away. You can see the bloodstains on the walls over there, though. And on the floor."

Now that he pointed them out I could see them, small brown dots spattered on the two walls at that corner, other dots on the floor, obscured by dust and sunlight. There had been chalk marks on the floor, too, but they were almost completely rubbed away, worn away, so that you could no longer see for sure where the bodies had lain.

I said, "Both killings took place in this room, is that the theory?"

"That's what it said in the papers."

There was a door to the left. Nodding to it, I said, "Where does that go?"

"Just another room. And then the bathroom beyond that. Come on."

He pushed open the door, into what had been a completely lightless room. The blackness in there was only emphasized by the long slender rectangle of pale light stretching across the floor now from the doorway. All I could see was that bit of blank empty floor.

Hulmer said, "Just a second." Going inside, stooping, feeling around at floor-level to the left of the doorway, he finally switched on another shadeless table lamp and the room leaped into existence. Windowless, with doors in three walls, it was empty in the middle and on the left, piled high with junk on the right. Cartons, spindly chairs, rolled-up rugs, all the detritus of life that has moved on.

Hulmer's shoes echoed on the floor as he crossed the room toward the door on the opposite side, saying, "The bathroom's over here. That's the one thing Terry had up here was water. No gas, no electricity, but anyway water."

"Hold on a second," I said, and knelt to study the floor at the threshold. But there were no brown dots, no streaks, nothing to interrupt the thin gray topsoil of dust.

I got to my feet, brushing off my knees, and followed Hulmer across the room. Either it was cooler in here, in the windowless center of the house, or I was just getting more used to the heat up here.

The bathroom was a surprise, modern and spacious and complete. The illumination again came from an old table lamp without a shade, but at least this time it wasn't throwing its stark light upward from floor-level. The lamp was on the formica counter beside the sink. Its light shone on beige tile walls, white tile floor, beige bathtub with frosted-glass shower doors, beige toilet and sink, a large double medicine chest with mirrors and chrome framing, and a white formica counter top with silver specks in it.

Hulmer said, "Not bad, huh? Kind of motel modern, but what the hell. Better than what *I* got."

"Very good," I said. I went over and slid open one of the bathtub doors. The tub gleamed in the light. Nonskid strips had been glued to the bottom in wavy lines. The faucet was dripping, very slowly.

Hulmer said, "What's that?"

"Faucet's dripping."

"It is? Never did before."

I reached in and tried the faucets and the cold water was slightly on. I shut it and the dripping stopped.

"All this modern stuff goes," Hulmer was saying. "But it was great to come up here and take a shower. You take a look in the closet there, you'll see stuff of mine, Abe's, George's, everybody's."

"Robin's?"

"Well, sure. They were shacked up, Mr. Tobin. I mean, that isn't exactly a secret any more."

"I know."

I opened the linen closet door to the right and saw towels, underwear, soap, socks, various tubes and jars and bottles scattered over the shelves.

Hulmer, irritated, said, "That's a hell of a thing."

"What is?"

"My Holiday Inn towel," he said. "My brother swiped me a towel from a Holiday Inn he helped integrate, and now somebody swiped it from me. One of those damn cops."

"No. Why would a cop steal one of your towels?"

Hulmer shrugged. "Why would a cop do anything? They were up here wandering around, a couple of them washed up in here, look how dirty they left the towel on the rack there."

"But why steal a towel?" I said. "It doesn't make any sense. You're sure it was here?"

"Positive. This is my shelf, my razor's here, soap, slippers, all my gear, everything but the towel. It was white, with a wide green stripe down the middle, and inside the green stripe in white letters it said Holiday Inn. And it isn't here."

"You're sure it isn't at a laundry or anything like that."

He shook his head. "I do my own laundry at the laundromat. Bring it down, put the money in, sit around and read a magazine, bring it home an hour later. That towel hasn't been away from me since my brother give it to me."

"Then let's look for it," I said.

He looked at me oddly. "Why? Why you so hot about the towel?"

I said, "The murderer got blood on himself, Hulmer. Maybe he used your towel to get rid of some of it."

"You think so?" He looked around. "What did he do, take a shower?"

"Maybe. And he was in too much of a hurry to turn the cold water all the way off. Unless one of you has used this room since then."

"Nobody's come up here except cops and now you and me," he said.

"So he probably took a shower, yes. And maybe used your towel to dry himself, and then to wipe up bloody footprints on the floor out there or bloodstains in here or bloodstains off his shoes. Anyway, your towel got blood on it, so he couldn't leave it around, because it would show there'd been someone up here other than the two dead bodies and Robin. Maybe he took it away with him, maybe he just hid it somewhere."

"The cops did a lot of searching up here. If they'd found a bloodstained towel, we'd of heard about it."

"You're right," I said. "So if I'm right and he did use it, he took it with him. Wrapped around his chest inside his shirt, maybe. But first we have to know for sure the towel's gone. You're positive there's nowhere else it could be?"

"One hundred percent," he said. "But what about the guy's clothes?"

"What do you mean?"

"He can take a shower," Hulmer said, "to get the blood off himself, but what about the blood on his clothes? He can't take them into the shower with him, they'll take forever to dry."

I said, "He wasn't wearing clothes."

"What?"

"If he'd been dressed," I said, "he wouldn't be that stained with blood. On his face, maybe, and his hands, maybe his arms, that's all. No point in taking a shower. But if he took a shower it's because he had blood all over himself. So he didn't have any clothes on. Let's go back to the bedroom."

"You want this light on or off?"

"Leave it on."

We went back to the bedroom, where I said, "I can begin to see the way it went now. The Boles woman was found naked, wasn't she?"

"Right. The hooker naked, Terry dressed."

"All right." I went over to the hall door. "The Boles woman and the killer come up here. They get undressed, they probably make love on the mattress over there. Then there's an argument, or a sudden passion, or maybe just the next step in a careful plan. Whatever it is, the killer stabs the Boles woman, kills her. Then he hears Terry and Robin coming up the stairs. No, he doesn't hear them, they just burst in on him. And there he is, naked, covered with blood, the knife in his hand. Terry makes a move, toward him or toward the door, and the killer goes after him. See, there's some chalk marks left over near the door here. That's where Terry's body was."

"Chalk marks?"

"They outline where the body was in chalk for the photos." I looked around. "All right. The Boles woman dead, Terry dead, the killer standing here with the knife. Where's Robin?"

Hulmer said, "Still in the doorway, wigged out."

"Right. In shock. She's watched a bloodstained naked man murder her lover with a knife. She's shut down, she's just standing here like a statue. The killer comes over to her, he plans to get rid of this witness too, but then he sees the state she's in and he sees a way to be sure the police won't be looking for him. He smears blood on her, he closes her hand around the knife, he leaves her there."

Hulmer said, "But what if she comes out of it? He's taking a hell of a chance."

"No. He can count on her staying that way for a while, at least long enough for him to take a shower, get dressed, clear out of here. Then if afterwards she claims some man did it, where's her credibility?"

"Some man?" he asked me. "Not somebody she knew?"

"I don't know. The Boles woman is what throws me off. Will you do me a favor, Hulmer?"

"Sure," he said.

"Look in the phone book for people named Boles in Harlem, call them, find somebody related to Irene. I've got to talk to somebody who knew her."

"Will do. You going to stay up here?"

"For a minute."

He went away, and I stood in the living room, looking around, watching it all happen, seeing everything but the killer's face. He was simply a pale force in the room, streaked with red, the knife glinting in his hand.

I could see the action, but I couldn't yet understand it. Why had he been here with Irene Boles? Why had he killed her? Why had he killed Terry Wilford? Why had he failed to kill Robin?

Did I have the sequence right? What if it had gone the other way around? He could have been here with Boles, Terry and Robin came in, he killed Terry, then had to kill Boles.

No. I'd had the death scene described to me, and Irene Boles had been murdered on the bed, Terry in the middle of the room. It had to be the first way, Boles and then Terry. Boles already dead when Terry and Robin came up the stairs.

Then was the murder of Terry simply an afterthought? Was it

the murder of Irene Boles that was the impetus of all this, and Terry's death nothing more than part of the cover-up?

Two people I had to talk to: someone who had known Irene well, and Robin. I had to know if Robin remembered anything, even in distortion.

I went back downstairs. Hulmer was on the phone, so I asked Vicki if she had a flashlight.

"Sure. I'll think where it is in just a minute."

It took rooting through drawers, but at last she found the flashlight and I went back upstairs. It took me ten minutes to convince myself there was no other way out of the building. The door to the roof was nailed shut, the upper-story windows were all boarded up except for the one in Terry's bedroom, which led only to the cul-de-sac at the rear of the building, and there were no exits into the buildings on either side.

Nor was there any sign of the missing towel.

Aside from all the other questions, there was still this extra question: how had he gotten away? The only way out was past George Padbury, and I was prepared to believe George Padbury had been telling the truth when he said no one had come out. He hadn't been the sort of young man to cover for murder, not the murder of a friend with another friend framed for the job. What he had eventually tried to call me for, and what he had probably been murdered for, was surely something much smaller, much subtler, which had only occurred to him much later.

So how had the killer left the scene of his crimes? He was up here, fresh from his shower and back into his clothes, the bloody towel in his hand or wrapped around his leg or around his chest, the two bodies there and there, Robin standing like a broken doll streaked with red, here by the door, the stage set, everything ready, nothing left to do but leave.

How?

Down the stairs and into Thing East, that was the only way. And he hadn't done it.

I finally gave up, for now. I switched off the lights on the second floor and went back downstairs, where Hulmer, elation evident in his face, told me, "I got you better than a relative, Mr. Tobin. I got you her man."

"Her pimp?"

"That's the one. He'll know everything about her, every last thing."

"Where do I find him?"

He said, "Mr. Tobin, I think I ought to come with you."

"Why?"

"Because this cat isn't going to talk to a white man and he isn't going to talk to a cop. And you are white, Mr. Tobin, and you sure as hell do look like a cop."

"All right," I said. "Come along."

"We'll go up in my car," Hulmer said. "I'll phone you from uptown, Vicki."

"I'll be okay," she said.

"Just keep the door locked till Abe gets here," he told her.

She promised she would, and walked to the entrance with us, and locked it after us. Hulmer told me, "I don't want Vicki to be next, you know?"

"I don't want anyone to be next," I said.

18

HIS NAME was Jim Caldwell and we had a hell of a time finding him. Every bartender Hulmer talked to sent us on to another bar, until I began to believe we were being sent on a snipe hunt, but all at once we walked into one black and crimson joint, the juke-box pounding away with the bass turned so far up and the treble turned so far down that nothing could be distinguished but the beat, and when Hulmer asked the bartender the same old question, this bartender leaned across the bar and pointed toward a booth way at the back, in almost total darkness.

We walked back there, Hulmer in the lead, the customers studying us with blank faces, and at the last table we found a tall, rangy, strong-looking man with straightened hair, slightly buck teeth, and a pearl-gray suit that seemed to glow in the dark. Sitting beside him was a dull-eyed young woman, plain of face, a trifle overweight, wearing a rumpled white blouse with long sleeves. It was cool back in here, but up front the sunlight was still an open-eyed glare on the plate-glass windows, and these two weren't dressed right for the day. In the man's case, the clothing could be put down to narcissism, the occupational mental disease of pimps. In the woman's case, the long sleeves more than likely hid the marks of addiction.

On the way uptown in Hulmer's ancient black Buick, he had told me the little that Irene Boles' sister had told him about Jim Caldwell. He had several women, Irene had been one of his women for three years, he had a reputation for a bad temper, he had no arrests or convictions that the sister knew of, and he hadn't killed Irene because he'd been at the sister's apartment for four hours that day, with three other people present, the four hours including the period when the murder had taken place. And the reason he'd been there was that Irene had run out on him and he wanted her back and he assumed sooner or later she'd show up at her sister's place.

It had been Hulmer's opinion, based on the sound of the sister on the phone, that she wasn't likely to be a party to manufacturing an alibi for the murderer of Irene. In fact, Hulmer had the impression the woman was sorry she knew anything to get Jim Caldwell off the hook. Hulmer believed there was no love lost between Jim Caldwell and the sister of Irene Boles.

Looking at him now, sitting at his ease in the back booth of Mighty Micky's, I was sorry he was alibied, because otherwise he was exactly what I would like for Terry Wilford's murderer: brutal enough to have used the knife, clever enough to have used Robin's state of shock to his own advantage.

I found myself thinking: Do you have the same thing in red?

Hulmer did the talking at first, beginning with a civil and slightly mush-mouthed "Mr. Caldwell?"

Caldwell preened under the Mr., and showed off a little with a white man in the audience. "That's me, boy," he said, his voice lazy and good-humored. "What kind of thing you want with me?"

"Mr. Caldwell," Hulmer said again, "do you know that little girl they say killed Irene?"

His eyes suddenly hardened into wariness, and in a sharper, faster voice he said, "What about her?"

When in Rome. Hulmer was talking now like a semi-educated field hand, putting on the dialect for Caldwell's benefit. He said, "This here's her cousin. He don't think she done it at all, and he wants our help." Half the consonant sounds were missing from his speech now, so that don't became dohn, help became hep. I could barely understand him.

Caldwell's speech was crystal-clear and hard as ice. "What kind of help you figure on from me, boy?"

"We was talking to Susan—"

"That sowbelly!"

"She told us how you were with her when Irene was getting killed."

Some of the hardness went out of Caldwell's eyes. He smiled thinly and said, "What do you know? I figured that bitch would railroad me sure, she got the chance."

"Can we sit down, Mr. Caldwell?"

He looked past Hulmer at me, and said, "Let the man talk for himself, boy. What is it you want from me?"

I took a step closer to the table. "Information," I said. "I want to know who killed Irene."

"That cousin of yours," he said.

I shook my head, and met his eye.

He wanted to be a hard case with me, but he couldn't quite do it. After a minute he looked away, and shrugged, and said, "What do I know? I was uptown, I don't know who she was with, I don't know nothing."

"Maybe you do," I said. "Let me ask you a few questions, see what we get."

"What do *I* get?"

"I'm not buying information from you, if that's what you mean. I'll stand for drinks, but that's it."

He laughed and said, "You're a cheap john, ain't you?"

"Yes."

"I'm drinking Scotch," he said, as though to impress me or scare me. "And my zook's on the same. Ain't you, sugar?"

She turned her head and looked at him vaguely, as though not sure he had spoken, or not sure he had been talking to her, or just generally not sure of things.

"Scotch is what I'm buying," I said.

"Then sit down, Mr. Cousin," Caldwell said, motioning at the seat opposite himself. To Hulmer he said, "Boy, you go tell the man we want him back here."

Hulmer seemed hesitant to go. I got out a five, pushed it into his hand, and said, "Get us a round. You and me, too."

"Okay," he said, a little doubtful, and turned away.

I slid into the booth, put my elbows on the table, and said, "The way I see it, Irene was the one he wanted to kill. The Wilford boy just showed up at the wrong time."

"Some fellas are unluckier than other fellas," he said. "But I'll do my talking when I got my drink in front of me."

"That's sensible," I said.

We sat there in silence, then, Caldwell grinning lazily at the empty glass in front of himself, the woman gazing lumpishly into the middle distance like a robot waiting to be turned on, and me facing them both, studying both their faces, wondering what I could hope to get from behind either of those masks.

Hulmer brought the drinks on a round metal tray advertising Rheingold beer. A shot glass of Scotch for each of us, a glass of water and ice for each of us. He put the empty tray on a table behind him, and sat down next to me.

I drank a little of the water and then poured the Scotch into the glass, filling it up again. In the meantime Caldwell had picked up the shot glass in front of himself, tossed the drink back, and put the glass down in front of his woman. Sliding her drink over in front of himself, he said, "There, now. That feels better. Go ahead and ask your questions, Mr. Cousin."

I said, "When was the last time you saw Irene alive?"

"Last time I seen her," he said. "Just like on TV, huh? That'd be 'bout five in the morning. She was out working, she come into the pancake place on Broadway there near Forty-ninth, that's mostly where I spend my nights. She come in, poor-mouthed me about things so slow. I told her things wasn't slow for everybody, she talk about how she feeling sick, she need a lift, I tell her she got to come all the way uptown for that, she can wait till six, maybe seven, depending how slow things go on the street. She went back out, she never showed up any more. I come on uptown seven-thirty, went to sleep, got up eleven o'clock, no Irene. I went on over to that bitch sister's place on Morningside, I'm still there when the fuzz shows up."

I said, "She was full of H when she was killed. Where'd she get the stuff usually?"

"From me," he said, surprised at my having to ask. "You wouldn't let a dumb molly like that make her own arrangements, she wouldn't never work."

"Then where'd she get the stuff the day she died?"

Caldwell shrugged it away. "From some john, maybe."

"That ever happen before?"

There was a slight hesitation, just enough hesitation, and then he said, "No, but that don't mean it couldn't sometime."

"You don't have to hold back," I told him. "I'm not law, I'm not on speaking terms with the law."

"Who's holding back?"

"You are. Irene connected somewhere other than you, one time, maybe lots of times."

Caldwell studied me, eyes wary, mouth smiling falsely. He picked up the second shot glass, threw the drink down his throat, said, "We're ready for more."

"Of course." I got out another five and handed it to Hulmer. "None for me this time," I told him.

He nodded and left the booth.

I said to Caldwell, "I realize there's nothing in this for you, and you're worried it might be dangerous to talk too much, but I swear to you nothing you say to me will ever kick back at you."

He nodded, grinning cynically to me. "That's maybe easier to say than to do," he said.

"You didn't kill Irene," I pointed out, "and that's all I'm interested in. If Irene connected somewhere other than you, why not tell me about it?"

Gazing at me, still thinking it out, he said, "Maybe because where she connected is some place I shouldn't ought to talk about."

"Like where?"

"Don't hurry me," he said. "Let me make up my mind."

"All right."

We sat in silence till Hulmer came back, bringing two shots, both of which he put in front of Caldwell. Then he said to me, "I'm going to call Vicki, I'll be right back."

"All right."

Caldwell watched Hulmer go away, and then said to me, "That's a sharp boy there, ain't that right?"

"He seems so."

"College boy?"

"I don't know. Possibly."

"Some friend of this little girl cousin of yours, that right?"

"They're friends, yes."

He nodded. "I come along too soon, man," he said. "Born just about ten years too soon. These baby cats these days, they go downtown, go to Greenwich Village, get themselves all the white ass they can handle. I try that, my time, I'd come back uptown in a suitcase."

"Times change," I said.

"She got it off some cop," he said.

The change of subject was too abrupt for me. It took me a second to realize he was answering the other question, and then I said, "The connection?"

"Right. Maybe three months ago, she was gone all night, come back nine in the morning, coked to the hair, tells me some fuzz picked her up by the Americana, she thought he was busting her, but it turns out he takes her to some damn cargo ship on one of them West Side piers. There was a fire on this cargo ship, there's nobody on it, he knows about it, takes her on, they go in the captain's cabin, shoot up together, they make it, she comes on home. Then like a couple more times the same thing, same cop, always takes her some crazy place he knows about, like he gets a kick out of being some place weird. Never gives her no money, but always springs for a shot."

"What was his name?"

"I don't know. That's straight. He never told the pig. Leastways, she said she didn't know."

"When she didn't show up at the pancake place that last morning, did you think she might be with the cop again?"

"Until she never come home. She was never later than eight-thirty, nine o'clock coming home when she was with him."

Hulmer came back, then, looking serious. "Are you nearly done, Mr. Tobin?"

"Just about," I said.

"I could use another round," Caldwell said, having downed both drinks during my questions.

I had one five left in my wallet and I gave it to him, saying, "If it's okay with you, you can order it yourself."

"I'd be more than happy," he said, smiling at me, and tucked the bill into his jacket breast pocket. His woman watched the money disappear like a hungry dog watching a plate being scraped into the garbage pail.

I got to my feet, saying, "Thank you for helping me."

"You think I helped?"

"I think you may have helped a lot," I told him. "And I still promise you it won't boomerang back at you."

"That's okay," he said lazily. "What the hell, I'm clean."

Hulmer was obviously in a hurry to leave. I walked to the front, he trotting ahead of me, and when we got outside in the humidity and the glare, I said, "All right, what is it?"

He said, "Let's get to the car, I'll tell you on the way." He started walking down the block, me beside him, and said, "Bishop Johnson called Abe, looking for you. Abe told him you might be at Thing East, so he called there, left a message. We got to get down there."

"I'm not sure we do," I said. "While you were gone, Caldwell told me something that just might be it."

"Let me tell you first," he said. He'd reached his Buick, and as he unlocked the driver's door he said over his shoulder, "Donlon's dead."

19

WE PARKED too close to a hydrant, at my urging. "If you get a ticket," I said, "I'll pay for it. We can't start driving around the block looking for a place to park."

When he had the car parked and the engine off, Hulmer said, "You want me to wait here?"

Until then I had, but once he asked me, it became necessary to have him come along. I said, "Why? Stick with me."

"Okay."

I didn't wait with him while he locked the doors, but walked quickly back along the sidewalk to the store-front entrance of the New World Samaritans building. I stared across the street as I walked, but of course Donlon was no longer sitting on that bench near the sidewalk. Two elderly women were sitting there, surrounded by shopping bags, talking comfortably together.

I entered the store front, my eyes took a second to adjust to the dimness, and then I saw Brother William getting to his feet from one of the rear pews. Behind him, Bishop Johnson was sitting, sunglasses on, looking grim and determined.

Brother William allowed himself a second of surprise when Hulmer followed me in, but didn't comment. Instead he said, "Do you want to see him?"

"Yes."

"Outside."

Three of us went out, Brother William first, me second, Hulmer last. Brother William led the way to the left, away from Hulmer's car, and most of the way down to the corner. He looked odd on this dirty street in his white robe, odd but clean. And cool. He looked as though the humidity stopped short of him, leaving him in a column of coolness and dryness.

He stopped near the corner and nodded at a black car parked illegally across the street, by the park. "In there," he said. "I'll wait here."

"All right."

We had to wait for the light to change, and then Hulmer and I went across and took a look.

It was the same car Donlon had used when he'd driven out to my house. The windows were rolled down and he was lolling in there, head back, eyes shut, mouth open. You'd have said he was sleeping, in the heat. Sunlight gleamed on the left side of his throat, and the flesh looked alive.

Hulmer waited on the sidewalk while I went around to the driver's side for a closer look. Just below the window the left side of his white shirt was messy with a gummy-looking brown stain, spreading out and down, across his belt, down into his lap. The gun lay in his lap, bloodied. I had no doubt it would have Donlon's fingerprints on it.

It was easy to see how it was done. Donlon had switched from bench to car, had been sitting here either still waiting for me to come out of the church building or merely keeping the church building under surveillance, and someone had slid into the front seat beside him. Not necessarily somebody he knew, just somebody with a gun. They'd held the gun on him, they'd taken his own gun away from him, stuck it against his chest, pulled the trigger. Then wrap Donlon's hand around the gun, let it drop into his lap, and leave.

No one would notice a single gunshot, somewhat muffled by

being fired inside the car. A backfire, they might think, if they consciously heard it at all.

Our murderer was fast, and an amateur, and improvisational. He had now murdered five times, and his MO varied widely from incident to incident. He had used a knife, a car, a heavy dropped object, and a gun. He had done murder that looked like murder, framing a bystander in the process. He had done murder that looked like accident, in the hit-and-run killing of George Padbury. He had done murder that looked motiveless, in the attempt on me. And now he had done murder that looked like suicide.

Where was he now? Who was he going to be afraid of next? Still me? Or were there others who frightened him also?

I had to talk to Robin. I had to see for myself how well she was guarded.

I walked back around the car to Hulmer. "I'll need to be chauffeured for a while. Are you free?"

He looked pinched around the eyes. "Sure. He's really dead?"

"Yes. Shot. I think it's set up to look like suicide."

"Why kill Donlon?"

"I don't know."

But my mind was taking it this way and that way, worrying it like a dog at a rag doll. When Jim Caldwell had told me about the strange cop who had fed Irene's narcotics habit and taken her unusual places to have intercourse with her, I had found my mind filling with the image of Donlon. He was certainly strange, he was hanging around unnecessarily, he had known about Thing East. But now I didn't know. Was he the strange cop, but nothing more, and had he too been looking for the real murderer of Irene Boles? Or was he tracking down the strange cop? Or was he something else entirely, his motives unguessable without more facts?

Hulmer was waiting for me. I was waiting for me. Months of inaction had made me sluggish. It seemed to me as though I should be understanding things by now, but comprehension was far away.

If only the weather were better, cooler, drier, less obtrusive.

If only I had more time. I felt as though, if I could have a day to myself, a full day to work on my wall and mull over what I had seen and heard, I would be able to put it together right, to say *this* is what happened, and why, and who. But the weather inhibited thought, and there was no spare time because our murderer was running scared and running hard and running fast.

Had he killed Donlon before trying for me, or after? After seemed more likely. There was more to think about in that, but I couldn't do it yet. I couldn't do anything yet.

I shook my head and said to Hulmer, "Come on, let's get indoors."

We went back across the street, where Brother William was waiting, his expression troubled. "You bring us violence, brother," he said.

"Not me," I told him. "I have my own retreat. This business forced me out, too."

"What do we do now?" he wanted to know.

"We get away from this sun. I've had enough of it today."

We walked back to the church and inside. Cool and dry. Bishop Johnson was still sitting in the same pew; he half turned when we came in.

I sat down beside him. "He's been shot," I said. "Dead, as you said."

"What now?" He seemed very bitter, very angry. "Trouble for everyone, is that it?"

"Not necessarily. I don't think any of us should report it. Sooner or later someone else will find him and call the police. We may not be connected to it at all, at least not right away. Maybe there'll be time enough for me to find the one responsible."

He pursed his lips. "I don't doubt your ability, Mr. Tobin," he said. "But I do wonder about your attentiveness. When you were here before your mind was divided. Is it still?"

"Of course. But I'll do the best I can."

"It bothers me to leave that man out there unattended."

"You wanted me to tell you not to report it," I said. "Otherwise, you would have called the police yourself first thing, and me second."

"Are you right?" He cocked his head, as though listening to something far away, and then nodded. "Yes, you are. Good. Your divided mind is nevertheless perceptive."

"I hope so. May I use your phone?"

"Of course. Brother William will show you."

"Thank you."

I followed Brother William down the length of the chapel and through the remembered door, the small conversation room, and this time into another small room with desk, chair, filing cabinet. On the desk were typewriter and telephone.

Brother William said, "If you can keep the police away from us, brother, God bless you."

"I'll try."

"Police don't understand the bishop," he said. "They look for evil motives in him."

"It's the result of their occupation," I said, and thought to myself that was an odd thing to say. Did it defend the police, or did it attack them? I wasn't sure.

Brother William said, "You'll want privacy," and went out, shutting the door.

I hadn't necessarily required privacy, but I didn't mind it. I phoned home and spoke to Kate. She asked me how things were going, and I said, "It's not done yet. I want to talk to Robin. Can you call her mother and arrange it?"

"I can try."

"And call me back." I read the number to her from the phone and she promised to call back in a few minutes.

I spent the time idly going through the desk and filing cabinet. This religious group was present in the situation, but not necessarily involved. They had provided the location, by rental, of the first two murders. The fifth had taken place outside their door. They had also been harassed by Donlon, in the same way as Thing East. Did their connection with the murderer go any deeper?

There was nothing of interest in the drawers I went through. Housekeeping matters, mostly: food purchases, tax affairs, insurance, things like that. Even a religion has its business side, and here it was.

The phone had not yet rung when I was finished. I sat at the desk and waited, and two or three minutes later it did ring and I answered.

Kate. She said, "I'm sorry I took so long."

"That's all right."

"Rita's going up there at four. She says two relatives are allowed in, and Robin's father was going to go, but he'll wait and go this evening."

"Where am I supposed to meet her?"

"At the desk. She says she'll be there at four."

I hadn't seen my cousin Rita Gibson for years, for so long that I couldn't manage to think of her as Rita Kennely, though obviously that had to be her married name. I said, "How will I know her?"

"She'll know you, Mitch."

"If you say so. Don't count on me for dinner."

"I wasn't. Be careful, Mitch."

"I will." I hadn't told her about the attempt on my life, it seemed pointless to worry her until this thing was over. Then it wouldn't be a worry, and I could tell her. No, then it wouldn't matter any more, and I wouldn't bother to tell her.

I wanted desperately to give this up and go home.

We exchanged good-byes, I hung up, and I got heavily to my feet and went back to the chapel, where Bishop Johnson was talking with Hulmer. Brother William was nowhere in sight.

I sat down next to the bishop and said, "Brother William told me you'd had some trouble with Donlon in the past. When you were in the old building."

"We did. He tried our patience sorely. We don't believe that God treats the world like a Monopoly game, so we don't believe that troubles are sent by God as tests of faith, but there were times when it did seem as though Detective Donlon had to be the emissary of something supernatural. The man's instinct for harassment was uncanny."

"Did you ever complain to his superiors?"

"That would not be our way."

"Passive resistance?"

"Say, rather, passive acceptance. We survived Detective Donlon's provocations, though with some gritting of teeth."

"Exactly how did he go about provoking you?"

"We have residents," he said, "several men and women for whom the world has been too much struggle. They have retired, perhaps temporarily, perhaps permanently, and spend their lives here in thought. It was Detective Donlon's practice to question these people, demand of them proof of identification, challenge the sincerity of their convictions, and so on. The same individuals would have to show him proof of identification time after time after time."

"How did your residents react?"

He smiled thinly. "In a variety of ways," he said. "Some with strong urges toward physical violence, some with sardonic fatalism, some with welcome."

"Welcome?"

"They were pleased at the opportunity to test their strength against a real trial."

"Did any ever fail? Anybody ever take a poke at him, or threaten to report him, anything like that?"

He smiled again, shaking his head. "Still looking for your murderer within these walls, Mr. Tobin? No, no one ever failed." Then a shadow crossed his face and he said, "I'm wrong. There was one failure. At least I attribute the failure in large part to Detective Donlon's harassment."

"Tell me about it."

"He was a man who had been a drug addict, and Detective Donlon somehow learned that. After which, of course, he would never leave the poor man alone. He was constantly after him for

names from his past, other addicts, suppliers. The man finally
fled us and eventually returned to narcotics. It might have happened in any event, but I have always believed that Detective
Donlon was the main reason for his failure."

"Where is this man now?"

"He killed himself. Many addicts do, you know. The purpose
of the narcotic is to create a wall against despair, and the day
despair breaches that wall the addict no longer has anywhere to
hide."

I said, "Are most of your residents former addicts?"

"Not at all. This isn't a halfway house. There may be one or
two at the moment, but the New World Samaritans has nothing
to do with narcotic addiction."

I said, "To be honest with you, I'm troubled about Donlon
being killed here, in front of your church. And the first two murders in your old church. Your group is bound up in this thing some
way."

"No mysterious way, Mr. Tobin. I believe Detective Donlon
was here because you were here and he had followed you. Perhaps the murderer in turn followed Detective Donlon. Brother
William told me that after you left, Detective Donlon went away
for a while and then returned. In fact, Brother William was afraid
he might have been aware of your departure through the rear
door and so might be following you again, after all."

"Was Donlon ever inside this building?"

"Not to my knowledge."

I shook my head. "There's still too much I don't understand,"
I said.

"I believe you know your work well," the bishop said. "I am
confident understanding will come to you."

"I hope you're right." I got to my feet. "Thank you for calling
me instead of the police."

"You already pointed out my ulterior motive in that," he said,
smiling at me.

"Thank you anyway."

"Would you call me if you learn anything?"

"Certainly."

I nodded to Hulmer, and we went on outside. Out in the sunlight Hulmer said, "Is he blind?"

"Yes."

"I thought so, but with the shades it was tough to tell."

"Is this the first you've ever seen him?"

"Yeah. Abe and Terry did all the business talk with him. Neither of them ever said he was blind. But they wouldn't."

"What do you think of him?"

"The bishop? I don't know, I guess he's a saint. If you believe in saints, I mean."

"Then you don't think the killer's somewhere in that building."

"One of the Samaritans?" He shook his head. "Not a chance, Mr. Tobin."

"I hope you're right," I said.

We got into Hulmer's car and he made a U-turn and headed uptown. As we drove by the black car containing Donlon's corpse, I saw a group of children standing around the curbside door, looking in the window, pointing, talking to one another, beginning to be excited.

20

ROBIN was in a room that smelled not at all of hospital. There was a bed, but nevertheless the effect the room gave was of prison. Bars on the windows, a uniformed guard at the door, flat gray walls, bleakness in the furniture and in the air.

And in Robin's face. She looked thinner, and the skin around her eyes was dark, olive with anxiety and something close to despair.

Despair was her cloak now, protecting her from the cold wind of reality. She tried to hide it, for her mother's sake, with smiles and animation, but the mimicry was flat, a poor counterfeit for the real thing.

It was painful to watch the two of them, the daughter pretending to be alive and the mother pretending to believe the daughter's pretense. I spent the first few minutes standing in the background, letting them have each other uninterrupted for at least a little while, and the shakiness of their portrayals for one another's benefit glared from every word, every gesture, every ripped smile.

Rita Gibson—no, Rita Kennely—was a total stranger to me. Nothing in her ordinary plumpish middle-aged face reminded me of any face from my youth. She had dressed herself in the sort of clothing that wage-earner wives buy themselves every fifth Easter, lavenders and pinks and plums which fade with the spring and are somehow gray despite their colors before the last of the Easter dinner leftovers are out of the refrigerator. It was too warm for the weather outside, so she had arrived looking uncomfortable and distressed, and now that added a note of irrelevant physical discomfort to the strain she was obviously feeling in her daughter's presence.

She had picked me out at once in the waiting room downstairs, and had tried to make small talk—the weather, the subway—until I told her, "We don't have to talk."

She looked at me with sudden surprise and gratitude. "Thank you," she said.

We had to be passed by a uniformed policeman outside the elevator on Robin's floor. He didn't like my presence, but Mrs. Kennely—I couldn't possibly think of her as Rita—assured him I was a relative, and at last he passed us through, with a white pasteboard pass for each of us.

Walking down the hall, Mrs. Kennely said, without looking at me, "I know you've had your own troubles the last few years, Mitch. I don't blame you for not wanting to be involved in this. I'm sorry I came to your house and tried to force you to help."

"At the time," I said, "I didn't think there was any way I could help. There still might not be any way."

"I'm praying," she said. "Morning and night, I'm praying to God to give you guidance."

We showed our pasteboards to the guard at the door, he unlocked it, and now we were inside, me standing as unobtrusively as possible in a corner while mother and daughter strained to hide their interlocking truths from one another.

Robin had barely looked at me at all, and I wasn't entirely sure she remembered who I was. When Mrs. Kennely finally said, "Dear, Mitch Tobin wants to talk to you, too," Robin turned her head and looked at me with the patient solemnity of a bludgeoned child.

I said, "How are you, Robin?"

"Fine," she said, in her thin voice.

It was a foolish question, and a mechanical answer, but I'd had to say something and I wasn't prepared. Actually, my main object in coming here was already satisfied: I'd wanted to know how well Robin was protected. The murderer was striking out in all directions now, terrified of something I couldn't yet see, and at any time he might decide he'd made a mistake in leaving Robin Kennely alive, a witness who at any instant might unlock the knowledge stored inside her head. He had taken a calculated risk with her, knowing that if she did remember the truth at some later date it was unlikely to be believed, but in the time since then he had perhaps grown less fond of taking risks. If he could somehow get himself in here, murder Robin in some way to look like either accident or suicide, and then get himself out again unobserved, then he could breathe easy. There would be no trial of Robin, no further investigation, no possibility that the witness would later remember the truth.

So I'd wanted to know the likelihood of his managing that, getting in and out of here, and it now seemed to me to be very unlikely. There were enough guards and enough checkpoints to make it just about impossible for anyone to get in unobserved.

Unless, of course, our murderer was a cop. The junkie cop, Irene's friend. Who had been involved somehow with Donlon.

But I'd think about that later. For now, Robin was standing in the middle of the room watching me, polite and patient and withdrawn. I said, "Can you talk about that morning, Robin, or does it upset you?"

She made a thin smile and shook her head. "It doesn't upset me," she said. "I just don't remember it."

"Where does your memory stop? When you went upstairs?"

"No, sir. I don't remember anything about that morning."

"Nothing at all? Not getting up? Not riding in the car with Terry and George?"

"Nothing at all. People have told me about it, so I know about it, but I don't really *remember* anything."

"What about afterward? Do you remember seeing me when you came downstairs?"

"You, sir?" She frowned at me. "No, I don't remember anything at all until I woke up here. I went to bed the night before, I fell asleep, and I woke up here." She smiled wanly at her mother, saying, "That was a scary moment."

I said, "Have any doctors talked to you?"

"You mean psychiatrists? Oh, sure." She frowned at me again and said, "Were *you* there? At Thing East."

"Yes. When you came downstairs."

"Why?"

"Why was I there? You asked me to come."

"I did? I'm sorry, but I really don't remember. Was it that morning?"

"No. The day before. You came out to the house. Don't you remember that either?"

"What house?"

"My house."

The mother was looking more and more distraught, and now she broke in, saying, "Robin, darling, are you tired? Should you rest? We can come back some other—"

"No, really," Robin said. "I want to know about this." Looking at me, she said, "I don't really know who you are. You do look familiar, but I don't remember ever seeing you before in my life."

Mrs. Kennely, her voice edging toward shrillness, said, "He's your cousin, dear. Your cousin Mitchell Tobin. You remember, the man who used to be a policeman."

I said, "You wanted me to talk to Donlon."

"Who?"

I felt a sudden chill. I said, "You don't remember Donlon either?"

Flustered, frightened, still trying to maintain the brave front for her mother's sake, Robin looked back and forth at the two of us, a scared smile on her face, and said, "What's the matter with me? Do I have amnesia? I remember *you*, Mama. I remember everybody. It's just that morning."

"And me," I said. "And Donlon. Why do you suppose you can't remember either of us? Is it because we're both policemen?"

"Are you a policeman?"

"I used to be. Do you know the name Irene Boles?"

"Of course. That's the girl they say I killed."

"Do you remember what she looked like?"

She shook her head.

I said, "Robin, do you think you killed them?"

Her eyes widened, the silence stretched between us, and abruptly she began to cry. She half staggered backward, her hands to her face, until she bumped into the bed, and then sat heavily and turned her face away. Her weeping sounded like metal ripping.

Mrs. Kennely was staring at me, wide-eyed, on the verge of some indignant foolishness. I made a hand motion at her which I hoped she would interpret as I-know-what-I'm-doing, and she subsided a little, watching her daughter worriedly, casting apprehensive glances at me.

I let the girl cry until the first violence of it was over and she would be able to listen to me, and then I went and sat beside her on the bed and said, "You didn't do it. I know that for sure."

She had lowered her hands from her face, but she made no response to me. She kept turned away, head bowed. Still, I felt that she was listening. I said, "The police don't know it yet, but they soon will."

In a very small voice she said, "I was up there."

"Yes. And because you'd gone into shock the murderer decided to let you live and take the blame for his crime. But it won't happen that way."

She said something too low for me to hear.

"What?"

"He said, 'Kill me.'"

"Who did?"

"The red man."

Mrs. Kennely burst in with "Mitch, leave the child alone! Can't you see she's—"

I waved violently at her to shut up, but it was too late. Robin had turned to face us, looking only pale and weak, once again bravely smiling. "I'm sorry," she said. "I guess I just have to cry sometimes."

I said, "What else did the red man say?"

She looked at me without comprehension. "What?"

She'd snapped out of it very quickly. Too quickly. Was there something unreal about all this? What if the mother hadn't interfered, how much further would Robin have gone? But of course the mother could be counted on to interfere, that would be the basis of the relationship between them.

I wasn't going to get anywhere here without browbeating the girl, and that her mother wouldn't let me do. Nor would I be able to get in here on my own.

I shook my head and got to my feet. "We'll let you alone now," I said. "You'll be out of here soon, try not to let it get you down."

She moved her hands vaguely. "Sometimes," she said, "all I want is for everything to be over."

"I know. It will be soon."

"Thank you," she said, with childlike gravity. The strange moment was gone as though it hadn't existed. She got up from the bed and smiled at me, saying, "I don't know why you're trying to help me this way, but I do thank you."

Mrs. Kennely said, "He's your cousin, Robin. I told you before."

"My cousin?"

"Don't worry about it," I said. "Family trees are very complicated and very dull. I'm involved in this thing now myself, that's all. So I'm helping you because I'm helping me."

That was the strict truth, but of course she chose not to believe it, and persisted in thanking me again. I was beginning to feel the same antipathy toward her as the first time we'd met, so this time I let it go and said, "I'll let you two have some time to yourselves now."

"You don't have to leave on my account," Mrs. Kennely assured me.

"I'm not," I told her. I couldn't help it, I disliked the woman, and one can never feel right about disliking somebody who's in trouble.

I started for the door, and Robin ran across the room to clutch at my arm, put her face to mine, and whisper urgently in my ear, "Don't talk to him!"

I pulled my head back enough so I could see her face; it was straining and intent, hollow-eyed. I said, "Who?"

"You know who," she said, low and significant, as though the walls might have ears, somewhere there might be someone who would spy out her meaning if she were too direct.

"But I don't," I said.

She flared up at me, suddenly angry, shouting, "Then go to hell! I don't care what you do, it isn't *my* problem!" She flounced away from me, into a volley of clichés from her mother, which she ignored, turning back to point her finger at me and say, "*You'll* be next, you know."

"Not if you help me."

"I'm out of it," she said. "I'm not going to get involved. If *you* want to make trouble for yourself, that's your affair."

Mrs. Kennely said, "Mitch is only trying to help you, dear."

"Then tell him to leave me alone."

"I'll talk to you both later," I said.

I had to knock on the door and wait for it to be unlocked from the outside. No one said a word until I left.

21

HULMER was waiting for me in the Buick, about a block from the hospital. He put away his paperback when I slid into the seat beside him, and said, "How is she?"

"Shaky. She's blanked it all out, the whole day. Plus me. Plus Donlon. Plus God knows how much else."

"So she couldn't help."

"She told me the red man told her to kill him. At least I think that's what she meant. Though she might have meant he'd threatened to kill her. That would make more sense."

Hulmer was frowning at me in bewilderment. "The red man? What red man?"

I quoted the exchange to him word for word, and said, "That doesn't ring any bells for you, does it?"

"Hell, no. Why should it?"

"Red man might have been a slang term for somebody in the group."

He shook his head. "Everybody gets called by their name," he said. "Besides, you said the guy was naked when Robin and Terry walked in, and all over blood from the other chick. The red man would be a good name for him."

"I know, that's probably what it is. But I could hope."

He grinned at me and said, "Maybe you ought to ask some-body else in the group. Maybe the red man is what everybody calls me. Why not? Put me in a loin cloth and some war paint, I'd make a hell of an Indian."

"I intend to ask one of the others," I told him.

He nodded, his grin getting broader. "I like you, Mr. Tobin," he said. "You aren't hip by a long shot, but you aren't square either. You're a whole different thing. You know what you are?"

"No, Hulmer, I don't. What am I?"

"You're the guy that said stop the world I want to get off. And they stopped the world, and you got off, and now you look at everything from off to the left a little ways."

"Yes," I said. "That's very good, Hulmer, you have a good eye."

His grin faded and he said, "Did I cut you? I didn't mean to."

"No, you didn't. Don't worry about it."

He shook his head, looking at me thoughtfully. "I don't know, man," he said. "I'd like to know what would make you blow your cool."

"August," I told him.

He laughed and said, "Okay, I'll let it go. Where now?"

"I want to talk to Irene Boles' sister. Will you phone her for me, set it up?"

"Sure."

"Her first name is Susan."

"I know," he said. "Susan Thompson. I talked to her before, remember? She's the one told me about Caldwell." He opened the car door. "I'll be right back," he said, and got out and walked away.

Watching him walk down the street, youthful, optimistic, hu-morous, bouncing on the balls of his feet, I found myself envying him in half a dozen different ways. I envied his youth, of course, and his optimism, and his humor, and I envied the absence of scars on his psyche that made the youth and optimism and humor possible. But beyond that I envied him for being young *now,* and black, and alive to the world in a way that I had not been for years, in a way that I perhaps had never been in my life.

I understand the motto of the new student rebels is "Don't trust anyone over thirty," and they're right. Between the child and the adult there is an opposition that cannot be breached or eased or ended. Neither side can truly comprehend the other. The child, as new and clean and efficient as a Christmas bicycle, faces the world with confidence and impatience, all his emotions gleaming like neon through the skin of his forehead. The adult, dulled and deadened and dwarfed by all the frustrations, disappointments, pains of living, faces the child with resentment and envy, insisting that the child be quiet, not make waves, not disturb the precarious balance by which the adult makes his small way through each cycle of twenty-four hours.

I was sure Hulmer and the others would not be pleased to know I thought of them as children, but that's what they were. The twenties are the transition decade; people enter them as children and emerge to thirty as fully embittered and wary adults.

Was it one of the children who was launched on this helter-skelter barrage of murder? Or was there an adult loose among them, his own emotions unnaturally released, his clumsy size wreaking havoc around him, like a panicky horse in a corral full of lambs?

I couldn't seem to get hold of anything in this mess. It was running itself differently from most investigations. In the usual case you have a list of possible murderers, a group of suspects, and you question them, study them, eliminate some of them, learn things about this one and that one, and at the end there's only one left, and that's your man. But this time I couldn't make up a list of suspects at all. I had a vague mental image of the murderer, naked and bloody, wild-eyed but calm, and no one I had yet seen came sufficiently close to matching that image.

I'd originally assumed that Terry Wilford had been the primary target, since the first two murders had taken place in his home, and so I'd devoted most of my time and attention to people who had known him, but now I thought differently. Somehow the Boles woman was the key to all this, and I knew far too little about her.

Why would anyone want to murder a Negro junkie prostitute? Had she tried to blackmail the policeman who'd been feeding her habit? Was he in fact the murderer? Or was there someone else in her life who had found himself compelled to end it?

But then why murder George Padbury? If the murderer was a stranger to Thing East, if his connection lay through Irene Boles, what could George Padbury have known? And how had the murderer gotten into Thing East?

And how had he gotten out again?

There was the rub, the pebble in my throat. If I could figure out how he'd gotten out of that building, would I then know who he was?

Donlon had known, I was convinced of that. Either Donlon himself was Irene Boles' policeman or he had known who it was. And he'd been killed because of his knowledge, because at some point and for some reason his knowledge had become dangerous to the murderer.

The door opened, startling me, and Hulmer slid in, saying, "Man, you were a million miles away."

"I was thinking. Will she see us?"

"Yeah. She said come right on up."

"Good."

Hulmer started the engine, but before pulling out into traffic he turned to me and said, "What I said before, Mr. Tobin, I wasn't trying to bug you. Sometimes I say things, they sound different from what I mean."

"I know that. Don't worry about it. Truly. You didn't offend me, and you didn't say anything that wasn't true."

Hulmer grinned and shook his head. "It's tough to do both those things at the same time," he said.

A child beginning to learn how to be an adult.

22

Susan Thompson, as neat and trim and compact as a lady golfer, let us into an apartment rocking with music. Smiling and nodding, she said something I couldn't hear, then shrugged and gestured for Hulmer and me to follow her.

We went down a hall, past a living room from which all the noise was coming. Glancing in, I saw four or five colored boys, late teens, hard at work on musical instruments: drums, piano, guitar, saxophone, perhaps one or two more. The sound was so loud you could almost see it filling the room. The boys were playing with such intensity that it was obvious their heads were full of recording-company contracts.

At the end of the hall was a swing door. Susan Thompson led us through there, released the door behind us, which cut the music to a bearable volume, and shook her head in resigned amusement, saying, "All those boys do is practice. You can't hear yourself think around this place." She had a faint trace of southern accent softening her words, blending well with her cheerful expression and matter-of-fact manner. "Sit at the table," she said. "You want some iced tea?"

"I'd love some," I said.

We were in a kitchen, tiny the way kitchens are in Manhattan, but as neat and clean and livable as a submarine. Hulmer and I sat at the small formica-topped table and watched Mrs. Thompson getting the tea ready. It made me think of home: coming in from working on the wall, sitting at the kitchen table, watching Kate make iced tea or, in the winter, hot coffee.

What was I doing away from there, trying to comprehend other generations, other races, other confusions and problems? This had to end soon, I had to get back inside.

We didn't try to do any talking until she was sitting at the table with us and we all had our iced tea in tall glasses in front of us. I took a taste, found it good, said so, Mrs. Thompson thanked me, and then I said, "You know I want to talk about Irene."

"I know." She glanced at Hulmer, then back at me. "This may be an awful thing to say," she said, "but I think it's a blessing."

"What is?"

"That she's dead. I know that's terrible to say, but it's true. The life she had—it's better to be over. Her sufferings are done with now."

I said, "There must have been very little in common between you and your sister, Mrs. Thompson."

"Oh, well," she said, smiling sadly, "not so much. We looked a little bit alike, except I was always skinnier. And I was lucky, that's all. I found a good man. Irene didn't. It's as simple as that in life, Mr. Tobin."

"I don't think it is," I said. "Forgive me for contradicting you, Mrs. Thompson, but I believe there was always something inside your head that was going to lead you to a good man and lead a good man to you. And I believe there was always something inside Irene's head that was going to lead her to a Jim Caldwell."

Her face expressed distaste. "Have you seen that man?"

"Earlier today."

"How did you like him?"

I shook my head. "I didn't."

"Irene doted over that man," she said, remembered indignation coloring her voice. "I'd ask her, time again, what earthly thing she thought she saw in him, and all she'd ever say was, 'Oh, Sue, don't you know he's my man?' *Her* man! Why, he's got three or four helping to buy those suits of his."

I said, "Were there any other men in Irene's life?"

"Men? There weren't *any* men in Irene's life, Mr. Tobin, and Jim Caldwell don't count. There wasn't nothing in Irene's life but that needle, and Caldwell, and sometimes maybe me."

"No other friends? No woman friends?"

"She didn't have time to be alive, Mr. Tobin. Irene had to work work work, and then fill herself up with all that drugs she was taking, and then work work work some more. She didn't have no life at all."

I said, "What about regular customers? Did she ever talk to you about any of her customers?"

She shook her head. "I didn't want to hear about any of that. She tried to tell me one time about some policeman gave her drugs, but I wouldn't listen. I told her, that life she was living, she could just leave it at my doorstep. *She* could come inside, but all that other trash had to stay out. One time she come around, she bring that Jim Caldwell with her. I was polite, I'm not mean to anybody if I can help it, but afterwards, next time I seen her, I said, 'Irene, I don't want that man around my house any more.' And she kept him away after that. There's never been any love lost between me and Jim Caldwell, and he knows it, I don't try to hide it."

I said, "He was here while Irene was being killed."

"He come around, he thought she was here. I was just as worried as he was, and I didn't want to have to call the police to make him go away, so I let him stay here. Then the police come around anyway, telling me about Irene being dead, and I had to give him an alibi."

I said, "As though he'd planned it that way?"

She looked startled, then thoughtful, but finally shook her head. "No, sir, that wouldn't be his way. He carried on here for hours about what he'd do to her when he caught up with her, and he wasn't fooling. It wouldn't be his way to try nothing like that."

"I suppose not." I shook my head. "I don't know what else to ask," I said. "She didn't have any friends, didn't have any enemies, didn't have any life outside Jim Caldwell and heroin and sometimes you. But somebody killed her, and I can't figure out who."

"I don't like to say this," she said, "but couldn't it be that your cousin *did* do it, like the police say?"

"No. Too many other things have happened since then." I drank some more tea. "No, the answer lies with your sister. There has to be somebody else in her life, somebody somewhere. An old friend from schooldays, a former boy friend, something. Was Irene ever married?"

"No, sir. Irene was hooked on those drugs when she was fifteen years old, and prostituting herself at the same time." She hesitated, then said, "I don't much like to talk about this, because I feel like I'm to blame in a kind of way. Irene was the baby of the family, you know, she was born when I was ten years old, and it never seemed like she could catch up to me. My mama was always saying, 'Irene, you look at Susan, you look see how Susan does, why can't you be more like Susan, when you gonna start acting like Susan,' all sorts of things like that. And naturally, being young myself, I loved that kind of thing, I showed off and acted snooty and all the time putting down my little sister. So she went out, and got involved with the wrong kinds of people, and that's what happened. And I sometimes think, if I was just nicer to her when we were both children, it all might have been different." She shook her head and picked up her tea glass. "But I think my mama was wrong, too, always holding me up like that."

"It's hard for parents to know what's right for their children sometimes," I said.

"Don't I know it. Yes, sir. You say to yourself, *I'm* going to do it different, *I'm* not going to make the mistakes my mama made. So what do you do? You go make some other mistakes all your own."

I finished my tea and said, "Well, thank you, Mrs. Thompson. I appreciate your spending the time with me."

"Not a bit. Anything I can do to help, just call, I'm always willing. And if you can find out who really did murder poor Irene, well, that would be wonderful. I mean, I know I say it's a blessing she's dead and all, and it is, but still and all nobody should have cut her up that way. Whoever did it shouldn't get away with it."

"I hope he won't. Before I go, would you mind if I used your telephone?"

"Well, sure. Right on the wall there. I'd let you use the one in the living room, but you hear that racket in there."

"This is fine," I said, crossing the kitchen to the white wall phone near the refrigerator.

"I'll give you privacy," she said, getting to her feet.

"No, stay there, I'm just calling home."

"I want to talk to those boys anyway," she said. "They got to stop practicing sometime." She hurried out of the kitchen, the swinging door flapping behind her.

I said to Hulmer, "What do you think?"

He seemed surprised. "You mean, did she tell the truth?"

"Of course not. She told the truth, as much as she knew of it. The question is, how much truth does she know?"

"Why ask me?"

"I'm talking to myself, Hulmer," I said. "I'm sorry, I was just using you for a sounding board." I turned away and started dialing my home number. I wanted to know if either of my police acquaintances had called in with news about a connection between Wilford and Irene Boles, and also if anyone else had called. If not, I would go home from here, let it jell in my mind overnight, and start again somewhere else tomorrow morning.

Behind me, Hulmer said, "I figure she knew her sister pretty well."

"So do I," I said. "Which complicates things." Then Kate answered the phone, and I said, "Hello, it's me. Any calls?"

"Mitch," she said, and her voice sounded odd, "there are two—"

"What?"

A new voice said, "Tobin?" Male, gruff, authoritarian.

"Who is this?"

"Detective Second Grade Wagner. Where are you calling from?"

"Manhattan. What's the matter?"

"Captain Driscoll wants to talk to you."

"Driscoll? Oh, downtown. What about?"

"I wouldn't know," he said. "Give me your address, I'll have a car come pick you up."

"That isn't necessary, I can get there myself. Where is he, out in Queens again?"

"No, at the precinct. You know where the Twenty-seventh Precinct is?"

"No."

"It's on Carmine Street, just off Seventh Avenue. West of Seventh."

"All right. Is he there now?"

"Yes."

I looked at my watch, and it was nearly five-thirty. "It'll take me a while to get there," I said, "in this rush hour. I'm up in Harlem. I'll leave now."

"I'll call the captain," he said.

"Let me speak to my wife again."

"Sure."

When Kate came on, she said, "Mitch? Is something wrong?"

"I don't know. I'll go see Driscoll and find out what he wants. Then I'll call you back."

"Mitch, Rita Kennely called, they've released Robin."

"They what?"

"She said it was about five minutes after you left, a plainclothesman came around and said Robin was no longer under arrest, the release papers will be coming through in an hour or so and then she'll be free to go. They're arranging now to transfer her to a private hospital out on the Island."

Something had happened, I wondered what, and if it had anything to do with Driscoll wanting to see me. I said, "I'd better get going, Kate. I'll call you the minute I find out what's going on."

I hung up and said to Hulmer, "Would you drive me back to the Village?"

"Sure," he said, getting to his feet. "You look as though something's going on."

"Something is."

"What? I mean, can I ask?"

"We can both ask," I told him.

23 ───────────────

HULMER stopped down the block from the precinct house and said he'd wait for me. I said, "You don't have to do that. I don't know how long I'll be in there, and from here I'm going straight home, and that's way out in Queens."

"That's okay, I got nothing to do."

"You've got Thing East. You're supposed to be working there."

"Let Vicki work," he said. "Sweat some of that extra lard off her. Really, Mr. Tobin, I want to stick around. I like to watch you work."

"Do you? I hadn't thought of myself as being very interesting or very useful the last day or so."

"You put yourself down too much," he told me.

"Impossible," I said.

He laughed and said, "Anyway, I'll stick around. What the hell, if Robin's off the hook maybe they've got the right guy now, that's worth waiting around to hear."

"All right, fine. Thank you."

"My pleasure," he said, and I think he really meant it.

I got out of the car and walked back to the station house. This one was dark red brick, four stories high, with black slate steps. It had probably been built around the same time as the one I'd been assigned to my last seven years on the force; at any rate, it reminded me strongly of that other building, and in walking toward it I felt the months slip away, as though none of it had ever happened. I was still on the force, Jock Sheehan was still alive, my double life with Linda Campbell was undiscovered, I had not been drained of blood and life and existence.

But I had been. This was not my precinct, I had to announce myself at the desk and ask to be directed to Captain Driscoll's office. The sergeant made a phone call and told me to wait on the bench across the way.

I sat there and waited. Two plainclothesmen came in with a short narrow ferret-faced man between them in cuffs. A uniformed officer left, distracted and worried, like a man who'd just been chewed out. Two plainclothesmen came down the stairs and over to me and asked me if I was Tobin.

I got to my feet. "Yes, I am."

"This way."

They took me upstairs and into an interrogation room, square and blank and nearly empty except for a few chairs and, on one side, a scuffed and ancient library table. "Wait here," one of them said, and they went out, and I was alone again.

It smelled wrong. They had both seemed wary with me, bringing me up here. And why bring me to an interrogation room rather than Captain Driscoll's office? And why make me wait again?

The answer was what they knew about me, ex-cop, thrown out, responsible for his partner's death. I would find no friends in this building, only memories, all of them knife-edged.

I prowled the room, restless and uncomfortable, wanting this to be over with. Robin was free now, and they wouldn't have freed her unless they'd gotten the right one to replace her.

Me?

I stopped, and looked at that thought. Could they think it was me? Was that why they let Robin go, why they wanted to talk to me, why they were wary with me, why I was in an interrogation room that reminded me uneasily of both my own past and that strange room where I'd first met Bishop Johnson?

They made me wait fifteen minutes, and when at last the door opened and five of them came in, I knew I'd guessed it right.

I said, "I was told Captain Driscoll wanted to see me." Though I knew I wouldn't be seeing the captain.

"Talk to us a little first," one of them said.

"Sit down, Mr. Tobin," said another. "This won't take long."

24

IT DIDN'T take long at all, once we'd gotten past the legal preliminaries. There had been a time, not very long ago, when I could have anticipated a fifteen-hour session in this room, being interrogated by teams of detectives in shifts, but the police are required to enforce more of the laws these days, including the ones limiting their powers and protecting those people—like me—who haven't been found guilty of a particular crime in court.

So I was told my rights, at length, and was advised to contact my attorney. When I said I didn't want to contact my attorney, one of the detectives said, apparently to one of the others, "It used to be they'd try to set things up for the trial. These days, they don't think about anything but the appeal."

The one who had been explaining my rights to me said, "I do urge you to get in touch with your attorney, Mr. Tobin. You don't seem to realize it, but you're in serious trouble."

"I don't think I am," I said.

One of the others said to me, "You think we're all here for fun?"

I told him, "I think you people are all here because you have a delusion. It doesn't matter what I say here, I'm not going to change your minds. And I don't have to call my attorney because a delusion can't do any worse than get me a few hours in a cell.

I'll even join you in your delusion if you want, I'll confess anything you want me to confess. But then sometime you'll get around to evidence, facts, objective reality, things other than your prejudice against an ex-cop, and we'll throw away the transcript of this session and forget the whole thing."

"You're sure of yourself, Tobin," said the one who'd done most of the talking.

"I'm innocent."

"Are you? Shall I tell you how we have it figured, Tobin?" Something had happened to the Mister he'd called me during the recitation on rights; I could see him memorizing that spiel from a mimeographed sheet of paper, with the word Mister and then ——. This time, —— was somebody named Tobin, so that's what went in there.

I said, "I'd like to hear how you have it figured, yes."

"Good." He pulled over a chair and sat down; the rest of them were still standing, scattered around the room like outsize chess pieces, all watching me, keeping their arms folded.

The talking one said, "You went there last Sunday, and George Padbury let you in and told you your cousin was upstairs. So you went upstairs, and you found your cousin engaged in perverted sex with Wilford and Boles. You've got a history of sexual problems, you couldn't—"

"What history is that?"

"We know why you aren't on the force any more," he said.

"I didn't know adultery was a perversion," I said.

He shook his head, unaffected. "I didn't say you were perverted, I said you had a history of sexual problems. Not every man turns his back on his duty for a piece of ass, Tobin."

I closed my eyes. "All right."

"So," he said, and I listened to him in the darkness inside my closed eyes, trying to concentrate on what he was saying and not what I was feeling, the eyes of these men—*these* men—who knew what I had done.

He was saying, "You saw the three of them at it, and you went wild. You killed the other two, but you couldn't bring yourself to touch your cousin. And there she was in shock, why not, with her own cousin going crazy in front of her, so maybe she wouldn't be able to tell anybody it was you, so you took a chance and let her live. But George Padbury knew the truth. You intimidated him, made him go along with your story at first, but you were afraid he'd tell the truth later on, so you killed him, too. Then you started making a big show about finding the real killer. That was partly to throw suspicion off you, but mostly it was to see if you could find some other patsy, get your cousin off the hook. Detective Donlon got onto you some way, so you had to kill him, too. You were seen near his car."

One of the others said, "That's the one you'll burn for, Tobin. That was your big mistake."

The first one said, "That's right, that's the one we're going to charge you with. Because there's no death penalty for murder in New York any more, Tobin. Not for ordinary murder. But there is for killing a cop. The cop killer still burns in New York."

There was silence, and it stretched, and they had to be done. I opened my eyes and saw them looking at me. I said, "Details."

"What's that?"

"The story's full of holes," I said. "Plug them."

"Show me the holes," he said.

"All right. First, this three-party sex. The fact that a young person lives in Greenwich Village doesn't necessarily mean he or she engages in group sex. I think you're going to have a hell of a time demonstrating that either Robin or Terry Wilford had any history of that kind of thing."

"We'll leave that to the jury," he said.

One of the others said, "You ever see the average jury, Tobin? You said it yourself, Greenwich Village. That's all the evidence we need on that part of it."

He was probably right. I said, "Next, blood."

The first one said, "Blood? What do you mean, blood?"

"Whoever killed Wilford and the Boles woman," I said, "got

themselves smeared with blood, they had no choice. Where was the blood on me? The first investigating officers showed up—what? —half an hour maybe from the time of the murder. If this was a spontaneous crime I didn't have any change of clothing with me, so where was the blood?"

"You washed it off," he said. "You used the shower, washed the blood off yourself and your clothes, came downstairs as neat as a pin. You left traces in the shower. And this."

He held his hand out, and one of the other detectives came forward, put a towel in it. He held the towel up and open; it was white, it said Holiday Inn in green letters, and it had a few brownish smears on it. "We found it," he said. "You didn't hide it all that well."

I said, "You have me walking around in sopping wet clothes and nobody noticing."

"Tobin," he said, "everybody's been walking around with sopping wet clothes the last week and a half. Who's going to tell the difference between a shirt wet with sweat or a shirt wet because somebody just washed a lot of blood off it? You can forget that blood business."

"How about George Padbury? He and I were present in a room with a dozen or more cops. Why didn't he denounce me?"

"You had him too scared."

"Scared? Surrounded by cops?"

One of the others said, "You told him you'd implicate him, maybe claim he did it."

A third one said, "Maybe you told him you still had friends on the force, so he better cooperate."

I said, "Do you people believe any of this?"

"We believe it all," said the one sitting in front of me. "You got any more holes for us to plug?"

"I wasn't near Donlon's car," I said, "until after he was dead. When the M.E. tells you the time of death, let me know, and I'll tell you where I was at that time and who with."

"You admit being near his car after he was dead?"

"Yes."

"And you knew he was dead?"

"I thought he was asleep."

"What? Now *that's* something I don't believe."

I said, "What do you want me to say? That I saw him dead, and didn't report it? I wouldn't say that if it were true." I held my hands out. "There's a quicker way," I said. "Give me a paraffin test. Find out if I fired a gun recently or not."

"It was an awful hot day to wear rubber gloves, wasn't it?"

One of the other cops said, "I thought you were trying to set it up as a suicide. Why don't you tell us to give *him* the paraffin test?"

"Because you will anyway," I said.

"That's right," said the main one. "We're doing it slow and careful and easy, Tobin, we're touching every single base, because we want you. We want you on ice."

"You're going to be embarrassed," I said. "When this is all over, you're going to be embarrassed."

"We'll see. Got any more holes for me to plug?"

"Let me think."

"Take your time," he said.

I considered telling them about the attempt on my life, the boy who'd been killed in my place. But they'd brush that off as coincidence, or maybe even try to claim it as another murder of mine. And in any case they'd make trouble over my not telling the investigating officers there about my connection with the Wilford–Boles case.

But it seemed somehow as though there was something important about that attempt. Or maybe about the fact that the boy had been killed instead of me. No, not instead of me, just that he'd been killed.

Had *he* been the target? No, it was me, there was no doubt of that. But when the boy died, that changed things, it changed something, it did something somewhere.

The detective sitting in front of me said, "Well? You got anything?"

I'd been a million miles away, seeing the dead boy, trying to understand what he meant. I shook my head and said, "Wait a minute. There's something— Just give me another minute."

One of the others made a comment, but I didn't listen to it. In order to be saying something while I tried to think, I said, "If Donlon knew I was a murderer, why did he let me close enough to kill him with his own gun?"

"He underestimated you. He thought you weren't any good except against women and children."

"They aren't children," I said, distracted, but I'd been thinking myself that children is what they were, these youngsters around the age of twenty, children just learning how to be adults. But they weren't children really, not in the usual sense of the word.

The only child who'd been murdered was that boy. Instead of me.

I said, "Oh!"

"What now?"

"I've got it," I said. "I know what happened."

"Tell us," he suggested.

I shook my head. "No, not now. You'll know it yourselves, after a while. You want to book me for the Donlon murder, let's get it over with. And when you know I'm innocent, then I want to see Captain Driscoll. None of you people, I won't say a word to you people. It's the captain I'll want, and I'll want to see him in the cell, and with nobody else around."

One of them, laughing at me, said, "What do you want to do, Tobin, fight it out with him, man to man?"

"No," I said. "I want to tell him who the murderer is."

"That's dramatic as hell, Tobin. We're all impressed."

"That's all right," I said.

The one in front of me said, "Is that it? You done?"

"I'm done."

He got to his feet. "Then let's go."

25

IT WAS eleven o'clock before I could be alone and peaceful in my cell. If nothing else happened in the meantime, I would stay in this cell until around noon tomorrow, and then be transferred to the city jail. I was looking forward to the intervening time, free of thought, free of words, free of movement and trouble and responsibility.

I had used my allotted telephone call to let Kate know where I was and what had happened, and to assure her that everything would be all right in a day or two. She had naturally assumed my assurances were false, had thought I was in more serious trouble than I was, and had insisted on calling Frank Kantor, a lawyer who has taken care of my few legal problems over the years. Frank had come down and had wanted to talk, had wanted to know everything, and I had wanted only to be left alone. I couldn't tell him what I knew, because he might not be able to keep from telling someone else, anyone else. The session had been uncomfortable for both of us, and went on and on, and he was angry with me when it finally ended.

I also had a meeting with an earnest young man from the district attorney's office. To him I was a piece in a fascinating game called Law; he had to move me safely in the direction of the electric chair without drawing any penalty cards from the Supreme Court. We discussed my rights at length, I assured him that no confession had been solicited from me and that I had been told at the very beginning of the game of the moves open to me, and he left at last with the satisfied air of a teacher's pet carrying a satchelful of neat homework.

In addition to the attorneys, pro and con, I was also run through an older and blunter and more basic routine. My fingerprints were taken, my picture was taken full face and profile, I answered all the normal questions while uniformed men at typewriters filled out all the normal forms, I turned over my wallet and keys and watch and belt and shoelaces to a thin dispassionate man behind a counter, and I was frisked thoroughly, head to toe.

I had been through all of this before, many times, but not in this role. In the past, I had been the one at the elbow of the suspect, the bored one watching the long childish process of each blackened finger being rolled on the paper, the quick callous snapping of the photos, all the little steps by which a human being is catalogued, stripped of his humanity, and converted into a prisoner. Watching someone go through it for the first time, bewildered and terrified, had always bothered me a little, and I'd preferred the tight-lipped silence of the recidivists. Going through it myself now, I fortified myself with the memory of all those others; we were an unbroken line, linked together, each of us saving a portion of self, all of those portions working together to make us strong, help us survive.

But of course I was sure I wouldn't be staying long, all of this routine was in my case a waste of time. How I would have felt if I were guilty, or if I were innocent but unsure of my ability to establish that innocence, I can't say. Less philosophical, perhaps, and more alone, and more afraid.

As to the two detectives who were now playing the role I once had played, their faces were expressionless throughout. But mine had also been expressionless, in the past, so it was impossible to say what these two were thinking or feeling or what their attitudes were.

In the middle of all this I was taken into a small room with a long table lined with chairs, where I was served dinner. It was like a TV dinner, except that the tray was larger and older and thicker and more battered. The meat beneath the gravy might have been some kind of beef. What the ex-cons used to tell me is absolutely true: prison food stinks.

I went through all of these things, the meetings and the red tape and the gray food, obedient and silent. I was done with struggle, for now. I had gone out into the world, I had left my hermit's cave, in order to accomplish a specific thing. That thing was now accomplished, or nearly so, and there was nothing more I could do until Captain Driscoll came to me. In the meantime I was going very nicely to be given—courtesy of the City of New York—a cell all to myself, a cave away from cave, where I could turn off all the motors, be away from all the eyes and all the words, and begin to restore myself.

Lying in my cell, on my back on the thin bunk, looking up at the gray metal ceiling, I thought for the first time in hours of my wall. I could see it in my mind's eye, straight and thick, the concrete blocks down in the ground below the frost line, the ditch down one side of the yard now and partway across the back, one line of concrete block in place, level and smooth. Once the ditch was complete, around all three sides of the yard and meeting the house at both ends, and with that one row of concrete block in place, then I could actually begin construction of the wall. At the pace I was working—and I was in no hurry to finish this job, having nothing to do once it was done—I might have the wall completed up to ground level before the first real snow of winter forced me to lay off and wait for spring. That would be interesting. I thought I would switch from concrete block to brick, about two-brick thicknesses below ground level, to allow for unevenness in the ground. And of course the bricks would be in two rows, with an open space in between, and in there I intended to put all the dirt I was now digging out of my trench. The whole thing was carefully planned in my head, and on paper, and in addition I had sticks driven into the ground and wire strung along the sticks to show where the trench had to be dug. The whole thing was being done with a great deal of care and attention and thought, befitting something as important as a wall. And when it was done, ten feet high, it would completely enclose the yard. There would be no way into the yard except through the house.

I was lying there thinking, seeing the wall in my mind's eye, when I became aware of someone standing outside my cell. The cell lights were off, but there was always light in the corridor, enough for me to get around the cell without difficulty and for me to see someone standing there by the bars, watching me, not saying anything.

I turned my head, and it was Captain Driscoll. I got to my feet and walked over and looked at him, and there was nothing to be read in his face. He was just studying me. I said, "Well? Do you know about it now?"

"Know about what, Tobin?"

"I didn't think it would be this soon," I said, and went back to my bunk, and lay down.

He said, "What are you so sure of, Tobin? And what's this business about seeing nobody but me?"

"I can't talk to you yet," I said.

"Why not? What are you waiting for?"

I didn't intend to answer that, so I closed my eyes and looked at my wall.

He said, "I'm here, Tobin. You want to talk to me, talk to me now. What have you got to say?"

"Nothing," I told him.

"This is your only chance," he said. "I shouldn't have come down here at all, and I won't be coming back."

I sat up and faced him and said, "You will be coming back, Captain. I'm not being a smart-ass and I'm not being smug and I'm not trying any kind of a stunt. There's a reason why I can't talk to you now, and the reason is you won't believe me now and I'll just have to say it all again later on. And there's a reason why when the time comes to talk you're the only one I'll want to talk to, and you'll know the reason then, without my telling you. There's no point in either of us staying up tonight. I'll probably see you tomorrow, or at the latest the next day. Until then, good night."

I lay back down and closed my eyes again.

I could feel him there, not moving, looking at me. After a while he said, "I wish I knew what you were up to. You're guilty, I'll swear to that, you killed Donlon and that means you have to be the one killed the others, and you're going to burn for it. So I wish I knew what you were up to."

I didn't answer.

A while later he said, "If this is the opening phase of some sort of insanity plea, I trust to God you don't pull it off."

I didn't answer that one either.

A long time went by, and then I opened my eyes and turned my head and he was gone. I shut my eyes again, and saw my wall. I saw it complete, tall, broad, perfect ninety-degree angles at the corners, shutting out all the world except the sky. Blue sky, pale blue, with small fluffy clouds in it. Pale blue sky, dark red bricks, green grass, me in the middle. Nothing else, nothing else.

26 ————————————

HE CAME back at ten-fifteen the next morning. I had breakfasted at seven, on cold pancakes and boiling coffee, and had sat in my cell ever since, wanting nothing and receiving nothing. The cell door was left open during the day, so the prisoners could stretch their legs a bit, walk up and down the corridor, but I preferred to stay where I was. A couple of my neighbors stopped by to chat and get acquainted, but I wasn't up to the intricacies of small talk and they got discouraged after a while and went away.

I was deep in reverie when Captain Driscoll arrived. He came into the cell and spoke to me and I didn't really hear him until he spoke again. Then I looked up and saw him there and said, "Ah. You got the report."

It was written all over his face. He said, "How did you know it? You could know you didn't kill him, but how could you know any more than that?"

I said, "Yesterday afternoon a large heavy object was dropped down a stairwell in a building on East Eleventh Street. It hit and killed a young boy of about ten. I was a witness. It would be Eleventh Street near Avenue A. Before we do our talking, I wish you'd check on that, maybe take a look at the sergeant's report."

He frowned at me. "What the hell is this?"

"Another victim of the same murderer," I said, "and the explanation of everything. That's why I don't want to tell you about it myself until you've seen the official version. Don't worry, I'm not going anywhere. I'll wait right here until you come back."

"You don't have to stay here at all," he told me. "You aren't in custody any more."

"I'd rather stay here, if it's all the same to you. It's quiet here. In your office, or the bull pen, or anywhere else out there, there'd be too many people around."

He studied me and said, "You're a weird one, Tobin, I swear to God you are. You won't talk to me now, is that it?"

"Not till you know about the other murder."

"And you want to stay here until we talk."

"If I can."

He shrugged. "It's your ball," he said. "You can make up any damn rules you want. East Eleventh Street, you say?"

"Yes."

"I'll be back."

He was gone an hour, during which time I tried to forget about the wall and get back to thinking about the murders. I had a lot to tell him, and it should be in some kind of coherent order. I had to know where to begin, and I wanted to be sure I didn't leave anything out.

When he came back, Captain Driscoll looked confused. "It's down as accidental on their books," he said. "You were a witness, all right. Why didn't you tell them at the scene?"

"Tell them what?"

"That it was an attempt on your life."

"By the person who had murdered Terry Wilford and Irene Boles? At that time you were still holding Robin Kennely for that."

He brushed that away. "All right, you were running things to suit yourself. You want to tell me what really happened there?"

"The two boys were at the foot of the stairs. I was coming down. They looked up at me, saw this thing falling, their expressions made me look up, I jumped out of the way, it missed me, bounced off the stair and killed the boy. I went up on the roof and he was gone."

"Who? That's the point, man, who is he?"

"He's the same one who killed Donlon," I said.

He looked surprised. "What? I thought you already knew about that. The paraffin test came out positive. Donlon really did kill himself. I thought that's what you were waiting for."

"It was."

"Then what do you mean, the killer's the same one who killed Donlon? Donlon killed himself."

"I know. And Terry Wilford. And Irene Boles. And George Padbury. And that boy on East Eleventh Street."

Captain Driscoll came over and sat down on the bunk, at the opposite end from me. In a flat voice he said, "Fill it in."

I said, "Donlon was on drugs. Every once in a while he'd pick up Irene Boles, give her some heroin and take her somewhere unusual to have sex with her. In the captain's cabin of a cargo ship one time. Odd places, as though the place itself gave him a kick. One of the youngsters at Thing East told me Donlon was always very excited by the thought of that second floor over the coffee shop, as though convinced there were orgies going on up there."

"Where do you get your information?"

I shook my head.

He said, "All right, the woman's pimp. Go on."

I said, "I don't know all that happened upstairs that morning. Donlon picked up the Boles woman early, I don't know where they went first, but they wound up at Thing East. Donlon let himself in with a skeleton key, any kind of master key, and the two of them went upstairs. They got high together, or maybe they were high already, but in any case something snapped with one of them or the other, and the Boles woman got killed. I'd guess she went after him first and he took the knife away and cut her up with it."

"There was a recent wound on Donlon's abdomen," he said. "It was in the M.E.'s report."

"All right. Then Terry and Robin arrived. Donlon was naked, smeared with blood, standing there with the knife in his hand, Irene Boles dead at his feet. Terry made a move and Donlon went after him. Robin froze. Don'on was cagey crazy, the way a man gets sometimes on narcotics, very clever and intuitive within a lunatic framework."

He nodded. "I know how that works," he said.

"So he used Robin instead of killing her, covered her with blood, put the knife in her hands, sent her downstairs. He probably took the shower before he sent her down, but maybe he took a chance on waiting till after. In any case, there was no blood on his clothing, so all he had to do was dress, hide in a dark corner, and wait for the second floor to fill up with plainclothesmen. Then out he comes, moving around with the rest, just another cop on the scene. I remember that George Padbury first pointed Donlon out to me as he was coming out of the doorway by the stairs, not as he was coming into the building."

"Is that why Padbury was killed? Because he realized later that Donlon hadn't come in?"

"I don't know. George tried to phone me about half an hour before he was killed. I don't know what he wanted to tell me. With Donlon dead, there's no way to find out. He saw something, or remembered something, and tried to call me. Donlon got onto him, was probably following him the way after that he sometimes followed me, sometimes followed one of the other youngsters from Thing East. I think up till then he really didn't think of himself as a murderer. The thing had happened, Boles and Wilford were dead, but that had been a crazy incident, it had developed around him, out of control. But for some reason he had to go after George Padbury and shut his mouth, he had to become a conscious purposeful murderer, and he wasn't fitted for the role, it went against the grain. He came into my house and talked to me when I had the youngsters there, and he was odd, just slightly erratic. In the middle of trying to pressure me out of poking into the case, he went into a soliloquy about loving children and being sterile. It didn't make any sense for him to talk that way."

Captain Driscoll looked surprised. "He was sterile?"

"That's what he said. Told me he used to think it was his wife's fault, but he'd been told by a doctor it was him."

"Maybe that's when it started. The business with the whore."

I said, "Before the coffee house went into that building there was a small religious group there. Both the youngsters at the coffee house and the people with the religious group told me Donlon was constantly coming around, harassing, poking and prying, seeming to have some sort of compulsion to assume the existence of dirtiness, filth. He was seeking degradation, straining for it the way a person pokes at an aching tooth, deriving pleasure out of making it hurt more."

He nodded. "Taking narcotics with a Negro prostitute was probably the worst degradation he could think of for himself."

"But it had to be in an unusual place," I said. "After all, Donlon was a romantic. Everything he did was done romantically, from the sessions with Irene Boles to the insinuating smirking calls he was making on Thing East."

Captain Driscoll looked away. "He hadn't been exactly right," he said, "not for a long time. I'd thought it was trouble at home. He wasn't on the take, you know. At least I don't think he was, though maybe lately, maybe that was another part of the degradation he was after. When I came to see you to ask you about your statement, it wasn't just to cover up a problem in my precinct, though I admit that was part of it. But I'd been vaguely worried about Donlon, too, and I thought you might have some answers for me."

"I didn't know him then," I said. "I don't feel that I know him very well now, either. His wife might be able to fill in some of the blanks for you. I think of him as a disappointed man, a romantic, blaming himself for whatever his failures were, working out his problems in strange ways, being erratic and troubled. Then he became a murderer almost by accident and it broke the balance he'd maintained, it set him up to destroy himself once and for all. For instance, I can visualize him getting a sexual kick out of smearing blood on Robin, loving the act of it, and then hating himself for it afterward, having it be just another thorn stuck in his mind."

"You think he was going to kill himself no matter what."

"I'm not sure. If he'd been arrested he would have tried it, he was definitely that type. I've seen them in my—" I stopped.

Captain Driscoll said, "All right, Tobin, take it easy. You used to be on the force, we both know it, you can refer to it."

"It's difficult," I said. "I'd rather talk about Donlon. I think the reasons for his killing himself are all the same as the reasons for everything else he did up till the murder of George Padbury, plus one more. When he killed Padbury he became a purposeful killer, and it was the purposeful killer that saw me slip out the back way from the religious group's new building, followed me, and tried to kill me. When he missed me and killed that boy, an innocent child, the one kind of human being he had uncomplicated love for, it was one item too much. I think that's why he went back near the church or whatever they call it. He came close to going in and talking to the people there, I imagine. It was between talking to somebody and killing himself, and he decided to kill himself."

He nodded. "It hangs together," he said. "And I see why you didn't want to try to convince anybody before we found out Donlon had really killed himself. But why just talk to me, alone?"

"This way," I said, "it's just between you and me. You can leave the case open, reassign the men on it to other cases, and let it be forgotten. Donlon's dead, there's no point making a public issue out of it. It wouldn't do his wife any good, and it wouldn't do the force any good."

He frowned at me. "Why this concern for the force? I didn't think you had good feelings for us these days."

"I didn't leave the force," I said. "It left me. Within my limitations I think I was a pretty good cop. I never had any major gripe against the force, and I don't blame anybody but myself for what happened to me. So if I can help keep the force from getting a small black eye it doesn't deserve, why shouldn't I do it?"

"I had the wrong impression of you last time," he said.

"I had you wrong, too," I told him. "I thought you were nothing but a precinct politician. I never had any use for that kind, and I still don't. I thought you were there for no reason other than to keep me from making waves, and I was disgusted by it."

He said, "Have you ever tried for an appeal or a reopening of your case? After a certain length of time, you might be able to get some kind of reversal, get back on the force."

I shook my head. "No. The board made it a permanent dismissal, with no possibility of reinstatement."

"That kind of thing doesn't always hold up," he said. "Do you have any friends left on the force?"

"I know what you're trying to do," I said, "and thank you. But I don't want to build my hope up enough to make the attempt."

"Why not?"

"Because if I start letting hope in I'm done for. When my appeal is rejected I'm a dead man. Another Donlon. Every man has his limits, and adapts himself to live within them. Donlon was pushed outside his limits once by finding out he was sterile, and maybe having some other problems, too. He adapted himself, he went a little crazy so he could go on functioning in the world, and then he was pushed outside the new limits by becoming all at once a murderer. And the second time he couldn't adapt, he was too far out there, too far away from himself. That's what would happen to me. I was pushed out once, and I've adapted, I've closed things down, I live small and move small and think small thoughts. Now you want me to push myself beyond those limits, you want me to gamble with my life, and I won't do it. I'd rather be alive, even if it's only halfway."

He studied me, and I could see him trying to decide whether or not to keep pushing me. I was relieved when I saw by his face that he was going to choose to leave me alone. He said, "All right, Tobin, I guess you know best for yourself."

"Thank you."

"If you ever change your mind, I wish you'd call me on the phone before making any moves."

"I will," I promised, though I knew I wouldn't be changing my mind and wouldn't be making any moves.

He got to his feet. "I don't suppose you want to hang around this place any longer," he said.

As a matter of fact, I would have preferred to stay in that cell indefinitely, but I didn't dare tell him so. The vast majority of people have worked out a whole complex of common attitudes to things, and whenever anyone has an attitude different from theirs they immediately assume he's sick or crazy, possibly dangerous, definitely incompetent to go on handling his own affairs, and they begin to meddle with him. So I stood up and said, "No, I guess I've been here long enough."

"I should think so. Come along."

We walked out together, through the locked door at the end of the corridor and downstairs to the counter where I'd turned in my belongings yesterday. With the captain accompanying me there was very little red tape, and I went through the outward process much more rapidly than I'd done when on my way in. It only took about ten minutes before we were standing together in the main front room, the sergeant's desk beside us, the exit straight ahead.

Captain Driscoll offered me his hand, and feeling self-consciously dramatic I took it. "I don't know yet whether or not we'll try to keep this quiet," he said. "I don't think that's my decision to make, I'll call the commissioner's office when I get back upstairs and try to make an appointment for sometime this week. If they decide to make it public, you may be called for the grand jury or the inquest."

I felt sure they wouldn't ultimately decide to make it public, since no one would be hurt by its being kept private and nothing would be gained by smearing the name of a dead officer. They'd have to leave Donlon's suicide a matter of public record, and anyone studying the case would be able to put two and two together and come up with the truth, but that still wouldn't be quite as public as page three of the *Daily News*: Love Nest Killer-Cop Slays Self.

Still, Captain Driscoll was still operating in the world and so had his fictions to maintain. I went along with this one, saying, "I'll be available if I'm needed."

"Fine. I'll call you one way or the other and let you know."

"Thank you."

Then I left, and outside, leaning against a parked patrol car, was Hulmer, smiling at me through all the heat and mugginess; the outside world hadn't changed since I'd left it.

I said, "You didn't wait all night."

"I called your wife," he told me. "She said somebody called her, told her you'd be getting out soon. So I called the precinct and they said you weren't out yet, so I came over. I'm supposed to drive you home, remember?"

I shook my head, feeling my mouth moving in the unaccustomed gesture of a smile. "Hulmer," I said, "you're something else."

"Why, Mr. Tobin," he said, "you're talking hip."

"I've been hanging around bad companions."

"That's right," he said. "The car's this way."

We got into his Buick and he headed eastward across Manhattan. At the first corner we were stopped by a red light. Inside, the car was like an oven. I saw an air-conditioned cab go by, headed uptown. The driver had a jacket on, and was smiling.

Hulmer said, "What happens now?"

"Nothing," I said. "It's all over."

"All over? They got the right guy?"

"Donlon killed himself," I said. "It was a legitimate suicide."

"Well, what about— Oh! You mean *he*—"

"It probably won't be made public," I said.

His grin was sour. "Sure not," he said. "Cops."

I almost went into a lecture, defending the police, but that would have been silly, and I refrained. I said, "Would you call Susan Thompson for me, tell her her sister's murderer didn't get away?"

"Sure. You want me to talk to Ralph, too?"

"Oh. Ralph Padbury, I'd forgotten about him. I think Abe Selkin might be best for that."

He laughed, saying, "I love you, Mr. Tobin, you're the coolest thing in this whole big city."

"I don't feel cool," I said, and wiped my forehead on my shirt tail, then tucked my shirt back into my trousers.

It wasn't too bad when we were moving, but it was terrible during the wait at red lights. At the last one of these before the Midtown Tunnel, Hulmer said, "What are you going to do now, Mr. Tobin?"

"Take a cold shower," I told him, even though I knew that wasn't the question he'd been asking me.

Fortunately he knew I knew, and didn't ask the question again, and we drove through the tunnel and out to Queens in companionable periods of silence and periods of small talk.

In front of the house I said, "It's been a pleasure knowing you, Hulmer. Thank you for the drive."

"It was a pleasure of mine, Mr. Tobin," he said. "From now on I do all my cop business with you."

"Good. Good-bye, Hulmer."

"So long, Mr. Tobin."

Kate met me at the front door with iced tea. "Did you get much sleep?" she asked me.

"Plenty," I said.

27 ⸺⸺⸺⸺⸺⸺⸺⸺⸺

THE HEAT WAVE continued for another two weeks. I did a little desultory work on the wall during that time, early in the morning or late in the evening, but it just wasn't digging weather and I spent most of my time indoors in one of our two air-conditioned rooms—living room and bedroom—watching television or reading or drawing new sets of plans of the wall.

Captain Driscoll phoned two days after we parted at the precinct, and the decision had been as I'd anticipated; no public announcement of Donlon's guilt. The investigating officers on the case knew the truth, and a few police-beat reporters knew it, and the people who'd been involved knew it, but that was all.

The day after Captain Driscoll's phone call I got a funny card from Hulmer Fass inviting me to stop by Thing East any time for a free cup of coffee—"ptomaine thrown in for nothing"—but I didn't answer the card or go back to Thing East and I didn't hear any more from the people there.

I knew Kate wanted to know what had happened, though she wouldn't presume upon me by asking. Gradually, over the course of several conversations, I told her everything I'd done and seen while out of the house. It all interested her, and I became too conscious of how lonely it had to be for her, sharing my desert island, and then I couldn't talk to her at all for a while. But that too eased, and at last we got back on the old footing.

I was restless inside the house, but it was better than the outside world. I survived.

The day the heat wave broke, there was a drenching downpour, rain flowing everywhere like water poured from a bucket, the sky gray-black, the world green-black, the interior of the house yellow-black. There was lightning, and wind, and sheets of rain. I prowled the house like a puma in a cave, and Kate spent most of the day sitting at the kitchen table, a coffee cup in her hand as she gazed out the window.

The next day was sunshiny, cool, beautiful. The ground was too wet for digging, but I could squish around the backyard, replacing the boundary sticks that had fallen, putting new string along them, cleaning mud off the tops of the positioned concrete blocks, checking the supplies under the tarpaulins to see that they were still dry. And the day after that, a Tuesday, was still beautiful, with the ground dry enough to dig in.

I was at it by nine o'clock, all my concentration at last returned to my wall. And at twelve-thirty Kate came out of the house, came walking across the backyard toward me, her expression troubled, and said, "Robin Kennely is here, Mitch. And her mother."

I looked up from the hole where I was digging. I said, "What do they want now?"

"Robin got out of the hospital this morning," she said. "They used drugs to help her remember what happened, and all the blank spots are gone from her memory now. They want to thank you, Mitch."

"I didn't do it for them."

"They think you did, and they want to thank you. Mitch, they're in the living room."

I looked at my work, but I knew it was no use. I'd have to go in and talk to these people, and they'd probably stay all afternoon.

Why couldn't they have come around during the heat wave,
when I couldn't work anyway?

I looked up at Kate and nodded. "All right," I said.

"Robin wants you to see that she's better," she said.

"I know, I know. I'll just wash up and then I'll come in."

Kate knew I was doing it only for her sake, and that troubled
her. But she wants me to talk to people, so she didn't let it trouble her to the point of letting me off the hook. She said, "We'll
be in the living room."

"Right."

She went on ahead. I put my tools away, went inside, washed
up, and went to the living room. Robin looked better than the
last time I'd seen her, not as good as the first time.

It was a long afternoon. They kept wanting to talk about the
murders, and I could no longer remember all the details they
wanted to hear. Kate filled in for me, did most of the talking, while
I sat and thought about my wall.

I got back to it on Wednesday.

NO EXIT PRESS

There is an extensive list of NO EXIT PRESS crime titles to choose from. All the books can be obtained from Oldcastle Books Ltd, 18 Coleswood Road, Harpenden, Herts AL5 1EQ by sending a cheque/P.O. (or quoting your credit card number and expiry date) for the appropriate amount + 10% as a contribution to Postage & Packing.
Alternatively, you can send for FREE details of the NO EXIT PRESS CRIME BOOK CLUB, which includes many special offers on NO EXIT PRESS titles and full information on forthcoming books. Please write clearly stating your full name and address.

NO EXIT PRESS Vintage Crime

Classic crime novels by the contemporaries of Chandler & Hammett that typify the hard-boiled heyday of American crime fiction.

FAST ONE — Paul Cain   **£9.95hb**
Possibly the toughest, tough-guy story ever written. Set in depression Los Angeles, it has a surreal quality that is positively hypnotic. It is the saga of gunman-gambler Gerry Kells and his dipsomaniacal lover, S Granquist (she has no first name), who rearrange the L.A. underworld and disappear in an explosive climax that matches their first appearance. The pace is incredible and the complex plot, with its twists and turns, defies summary.

SEVEN SLAYERS — Paul Cain £3.99pb, £9.95hb
A superb collection of seven stories about seven star crossed killers and the sole follow up to the very successful Fast One. Peopled by racketeers, con men, dope pushers, private detectives, cops, newspapermen and women of some virtue or none at all. Seven Slayers is as intense a 'noir' portrait of depression era America as those painted by Horace McCoy and James M Cain.

THE DEAD DON'T CARE — Jonathan Latimer £3.95pb, £9.95hb
Meet Bill Crane, the hard-boiled P.I., and his two sidekicks, O'Malley and Doc Williams. The locale of the cyclonic action is a large Florida estate near Miami. A varied cast includes a former tragic actress turned dipso, a gigolo, a 'Babe' from Minsky's, a broken down welterweight and an exotic Mayan dancer. Kidnapping and murder give the final shake to the cocktail and provide an explosive and shocking climax.

THE LADY IN THE MORGUE — Jonathan Latimer £3.99pb, £9.95hb

Crime was on the up. People sang of Ding-Dong Daddy, skirts were long and lives were short, violin cases mostly sported machine guns. Bill Crane thought it was a pretty wonderful time. He was in the Chicago morgue at the height of summer, trying to cool off and learn the identity of its most beautiful inmate. So-called Alice Ross had been found hanging, absolutely naked, in the room of a honky tonk hotel. His orders were to find out whc she really was. Alice was stolen from her slab that night! Thus began the crazy hunt for a body and a name, through lousy hotels, dancehalls and penthouses, with occasional side trips to bed to bar to blonde and back again.

MURDER IN THE MADHOUSE — Jonathan Latimer £3.99pb, £9.95hb

Hard drinking, hard living Bill Crane in his first case has himself committed incognito to a private sanitarium for the mentally insane to protect rich, little Ms Van Camp. Terror, violence and sudden death follow when a patient is found strangled with a bathrobe cord. The murderer strikes again but makes a fatal error in killing pleasant little mute, Mr Penny. The local police doubt Crane is a bonafide detective and believe he is suffering from delusions, the non-alcoholic kind. Despite all this, Crane breaks the case in a final scene of real dramatic fury.

HEADED FOR A HEARSE — Jonathan Latimer £3.99pb, £9.95hb

Death row, Chicago county jail. Robert Westland, convicted of his wife's murder, is six days from the 'chair'. What seems an iron clad case against Westland begins to fall apart as Bill Crane races against time to investigate the background of the major players and prove Westland's innocence. Westland's two brokerage partners; his hard drinking, hard riding cousin; enigmatic and exotic Ms Brentino; the amiable Ms Hogan; a secretive clerk; a tight-lipped valet and a dipso widow all have plenty to explain. Aided by a lime squeezer, a quart of whisky, a monkey wrench, a taxi cab, a stop watch and a deep sea diver, Crane cracks the case in this locked room classic.

GREEN ICE — Raoul Whitfield £3.99pb, £9.95hb

Watch out for Mal Ourney: where Mal goes, murder follows. It is on his heels as he walks out of Sing Sing after taking a manslaughter rap for a dubious dame and follows him all the way on the trail of some sizzling hot emeralds — 'Green Ice'. "naked action pounded into tough compactness by staccato, hammer-like writing" Dashiell Hammett.

DEATH IN A BOWL — Raoul Whitfield £3.99pb, £9.95hb

Maestro Hans Reiner is on the podium, taking the fiddle players through a big crescendo. Then something goes off with a bang and it isn't the tympani! Reiner finds himself with a load of lead in the back — and a new tune: The Funeral March.

THE VIRGIN KILLS — Raoul Whitfield £3.99pb, £9.95hb

Millionaire gambler Eric Vennel's yacht sets sail for the regatta at Poughkeepsie with an oddball assortment of uneasy companions: Hardheaded sportswriter Al Conners; beautiful Hollywood ham, Carla Sard; Sard's nemesis tart-tongued scribbler Rita Veld; big ugly out of place bruiser Mick O'Rourke, and a glittering cross-section of east and west coast society. Rumours of Vennel's heavy betting on the regatta and a midnight attack by a masked intruder raise the tension . . . to the point of murder!

HALO IN BLOOD — Howard Browne £3.99pb, £9.95hb

Meet Paul Pine, Chicago P.I. Three seemingly unrelated events — the funeral of a pauper at which 12 clergymen from different faiths are the only mourners; Pine being hired by John Sandmark to dig up some dirt on the man intending to marry his daughter, Leona; and a run-in with the gangster, D'Allemand, where Pine is nearly killed delivering a $25,000 ransom in counterfeit bills — are woven into a complex and web of events that produces some explosive twists to the finale.

HALO FOR SATAN — Howard Browne £3.99pb, £9.95hb.

Raymond Wirtz has something everyone wants! His grace, the Bishop of Chicago; Lola North, "a girl who could turn out to be as pure as an easter lily or steeped in sin and fail to surprise you either way"; Louis Antuni, Chicago Godfather; Constance Benbrook, who "wasn't the type to curl up with anything as inanimate as a novel" and mysterious super criminal, Jafar Baijan — all want what Wirtz has . . . the ultimate religious artefact. Private Eye, Paul Pine is right in the middle. In the middle of a deadly obstacle race strewn with corpses, cops and beautiful women.

RED GARDENIAS — Jonathan Latimer £2.99pb

Bill Crane's fifth and final mystery finds him teamed up again with Doc Williams and Ann Fortune, his boss's niece, who poses as his wife, to investigate a murder and a death threat to the family of an industrial magnate. On the way to cracking the case in his own, inimitable way he learns the secret of the gardenia perfume, the lipstick marks on the dead man's face, the crimson cat, the three shelves and the hairpin! Latimer's deft blending of humour and suspense has been described as "masterful — the proper proportion of dry vermouth to produce a fine martini, all without bruising the gin!"

BLUES FOR A PRINCE — Bart Spicer £2.99pb

The Prince was dead. Harold Morton Prince, great jazz and blues composer had been killed in the studio of his sprawling, palatial home. From coast to coast, the papers carried his life story and every band was playing his blues pieces. But already ugly rumours threatened his name. Carney Wilde, P.I., had reasons to doubt the official story of how The Prince died and they centred on the people closest to him: His daughter Martha, his musician colleagues, The Prince's patient and dying father and the deadly Hollie Gray. Threads from each of these led Wilde along the dark road to the killer.

NO EXIT PRESS Contemporary Crime

A companion to Vintage Crime in the popular pocket book format that highlights both the classic and exciting new books from the past twenty years of American Crime Fiction. Contemporary Crime will feature in 1989 such titles as Day of the Ram by William Campbell Gault, Ask the Right Question by Michael Z Lewin, Act of Fear by Michael Collins, Dead Ringer and Castles Burning by Arthur Lyons all costing just £2.99.

ACT OF FEAR — Michael Collins £2.99

Act of Fear won an Edgar for the best first novel and introduces
the one-armed New York City detective, Dan Fortune.
Two seemingly simple events — the mugging of a policeman and
the disappearance of a neighbourhood youth, a possible witness
— inexorably lead Fortune to a more serious matter as one of
the witness's friends, a kid, hires Dan to find the missing boy.
Two girls, an innocent old man are murdered and Fortune's client
lands up in hospital. Then the killers go after Dan and he finds
himself in the middle of a bitter dispute between rival Mafia
factions.
"A notable writing talent" Ross Macdonald.

THREE WITH A BULLET — Arthur Lyons £2.99

A top LA music promoter hires Jacob Asch to find out who is
methodically trying to destroy him by cancelling appointments and
bookings. Then a faded superstar is found dead — apparently
from a drug overdose — and the promoter is the prime suspect.
Then two more bodies surface. Asch enters the glitzy, frenzied,
music world where the sex, drugs and rock 'n' roll combine with
ruthlessly competitive professional ambitions to create a murderous
mixture.
"Lyons writes with grace and energy" John D. MacDonald.
"Lyons belongs up there with . . . Ross Macdonald" New York
Times.
"Some of the best side of the mouth similes this side of Chandler"
Newsweek.

CASTLES BURNING — Arthur Lyons £2.99

A young L.A. artist hires Jacob Asch to track down the wife and
infant son he deserted years ago to make amends, now he has
made good. Asch finds her in the plush sybaritic world of Palm
Springs, remarried to a wealthy businessman. He finds the son
was killed in a car crash, driven by his mother. The case seems
closed until the teenage son of her second marriage is kidnapped
and Asch's client mysteriously disappears.
"Lyons writes with grace and energy" John D. MacDonald.
"Lyons belongs up there with . . . Ross Macdonald" New York
Times.
"Some of the best side of the mouth similes this side of Chandler"
Newsweek.

HARD TRADE — Arthur Lyons £2.99pb
LA's most renowned detective, Jacob Asch is on the street once more in a startling tale of Californian political corruption. A troubled woman hires Asch to uncover the truth about the man she is to marry. When Asch discovers the man is gay and the woman is run down on her way to a hastily called meeting with Asch, it becomes clear something big is at stake. Serious money real estate schemes, the seamy side of LA gay life and a murder frame involve Asch in a major political scandal that costs him his licence and nearly his life.

THE KILLING FLOOR — Arthur Lyons £2.99pb
David Fein, owner of Supreme Packing, a slaughterhouse in a grimy little Californian town had a problem . . . he was a compulsive gambler. First he couldn't cover his losses from the takings so he got a loan and went into debt. By the time he took in Tortorello, a clean cut Harvard type but with 'Family' connections he was in big trouble. Now he had been missing for 4 days and his wife was frantic. Jake Bloom, old family friend puts her in touch with Jacob Asch, who figures Fein is on a bender or in the sack with another woman — he's heard and seen it all before. But that's before he finds a body on the killing floor.

DEAD RINGER — Arthur Lyons £2.99
Jacob Asch is called in by boxing promoter Jack Schwartz to help out Carlos Realango, a South American heavyweight whose career is on the skids. He has been receiving threatening phone calls and Susan Mezzano his manager and mistress thinks her husband is responsible. Asch shows them how to tap their own phone and leaves it at that. Two weeks later Asch is called to Reno to prevent Realango tearing the husband apart only to find it is too late as Realango has been shot at Moonfire ranch, a fancy brothel, owned by the husband. The police say justifiable homicide, but Asch smells murder and something more than a lovers' quarrel.
''Lyons belongs up there with . . . Ross Macdonald'' New York Times.

THE LADY IN THE CAR WITH GLASSES AND A GUN —
Sebastian Japrisot £2.99

Dany Longo is 26, blonde, beautiful and short-sighted. After borrowing her employer's car to drive to the south of France, she is confronted with one terrifying incident after another. She is handed the coat she forgot yesterday, the garage man checks the car he repaired the day before and a policeman asks her if she got back to Paris on time the previous night . . . when she had been there all day!

When she is attacked, her glasses smashed, her hand crushed and then she is confronted by a man in the boot of her car, Dany belives she is going mad. Japrisot brilliantly developes this into a tangled mystery story that won 'Le Prix d'Honneur' when first published.

NO EXIT CRIME CUTS brings the very best in crime writing, old and new at unbeatably low prices!

FAST ONE — Paul Cain (New Edition) £1.99

WAX APPLE — Tucker Coe (aka Donald Westlake) £1.99

Mitch Tobin, ex NYPD policeman was sacked for neglect that resulted in the death of his partner and friend. Racked by guilt, Tobin retires into a grim artificial world of his own until he is drawn out to investigate a series of suspicious fatal accidents at the Midway sanatorium. Five minutes after arriving Tobin is a victim himself, left with a broken arm, a headache and no idea where to begin. Then the fire escape collapses and the dirty game becomes murder!

LITTLE CAESAR — W. R. Burnett £1.99

CHICAGO. Girls and pimps, bootleggers and booze, killers and 'typewriters'. Go down the mean dark streets and see the cats sniffing the corpes. Go down the alleys and meet Rico, and Otero, Bat Carillo and Baa Baa Otavio, Killer Pepi and Kidney Bean. There are the squirrels, flapping to stay alive – Blondy Belle and Seal-Skin, Blue Jay and Olga. All playing for power. All certain to die! Little Caesar is the prototype underworld novel that inspired a whole generation of gangster films.

BURGLARS CAN'T BE CHOOSERS — Lawrence Block £1.99

Introducing Bernie Rhodenbarr, New York City's prince of thieves – who really should have known better!

When the mysterious pear-shaped man with a lot of uncomfortably accurate information about Bernie and his career offered him 5 big ones to liberate a blue leather box – unopened – it would have been a good time to plead a previous engagement, but times were tough. Everything was straightforward until two men in blue coats arrived before the liberation. Still all was not lost, there was always a way to work things out – but then they discover the body in the bedroom!

NO EXIT PRESS

MATCH ME SIDNEY –
The 1990 No Exit Press Crime Compendium

A Marvellous mix of all things NO EXIT! Features a full length novel by Cornell Woolrich (Phantom Lady – filmed with Franchot Tone), short stories by Stanley Ellin, Max Allan Collins, Loren Estelman, Sue Grafton, John Lutz, Arthur Lyons, Michael Z Lewin, Paul Cain, Bill Pronzini and many others. In addition there is the Murder One Top 30 books of the year, the 1990 No Exit Press Crime Diary, the No Exit Prize Crime Crossword plus much more.
592pp/Crime Fiction/£8.95pb/216x135mm/0 948353 59 7/November 1989

Barry Came
RICE WINE

Paul Stenmark is sent by a Washington agency to a village in Luzon in the Philippines during the last years of the Marcos era to determine whether to fund a new dam project.
Fr Frank Enright and village elder Alfredo Dantog aided by the communist insurgents led by Ka Larry, oppose the project while Marcos stooge, Lt Col Rosales is eager to push the project through. All these elements combine against the backdrop of a terrifying monsoon to make for a tremendous adventure thriller with elements of Robert Stone, Wilber Smith and Philip Caputo.
'... a riveting story, told with sure skill and charged with insight. It is a novel of passion and Politics, of American innocence abroad and of the victims of that innocence. Full blooded and fully realised, it is at once highly readable entertainment and an important work, one which takes the reader beyond the international headlines for a behind the scenes look at the morality play being staged in developing countries throughout the world' – **Nicholas Proffitt** (author of *Gardens of Stone*)
304pp / Fiction / £3.99pb / 178x111mm ('A' format) / 0 948353 58 9/ January 1990

Lawrence Block
THE BURGLAR IN THE CLOSET

Bernie Rhodenbarr, introduced in *Burglars can't be Choosers* (available from No Exit) is back. The so-called professional has got himself locked in the clothes cupboard of a smart New York apartment, while thieving it. And there was his swag all neatly packed, not in hand and not at hand but on the opposite side of the bedroom! By the time Bernie has picked the lock he was not best pleased to find the loot gone and more alarmingly the beautiful owner, Crystal Sheldrake lying very dead in their former resting place!
192pp/Crime Fiction/£3.50pb/'A' format/0 948353 70 8/June 1990

Sebastien Japrisot

10.30 FROM MARSEILLES
TRAP FOR CINDERELLA

Two more classic sixties thrillers from Japrisot, whose new novel *Women in Evidence* is to be published by Secker. *10.30 from Marseilles* was Japrisot's first novel and is an excellent example of the police procedural. It was filmed starring Yves Montand and Simone Signoret. *Trap for Cinderella* is an exceedingly complex psychological thriller that won the Grand Prix de la Litterature de Policiere, similar in style to *The Lady in the Car with Glasses and a Gun*, also published by No Exit.

256pp/Crime Fiction/£3.99 each/'A' format/0 948353 73 2 *(10.30 Marseilles)*, 79 1 *(Trap for Cinderella)/*
March 1990.

Arthur Lyons

THE DEAD ARE DISCREET

Asch is back on the trail, investigating the gruesome murders of socialite Shiela Warren and her boyfriend, film producer, Randy Folsom. All clues point to Shiela's distraught husband as the killer. Then Asch discovers Shiela has been dabbling in witchcraft prior to her death and then of a porno film starring Shiela now in the hands of an arcane set of Satanists, whose uncanny rites suggest a completely different motive for the crime.
'The best L.A. detective novel of the year' – **Los Angeles Times**
224pp/Crime Fiction/£3.50pb/'A' format/0 948353 72 4/June 1990

Stuart Kaminsky

BURIED CAESARS

Hollywood P.I., Toby Peters in his 13th case receives a call from General Douglas MacArthur who wants Peters to investigate the theft, by one of his own aides, of some papers and campaign funds, that will destroy the General's budding political career. Peters is helped by one Dashiell Hammett, an ex Pinkerton man looking to kill some time in sunny California. The aide turns up dead and they trace it back to the mysterious Mr Pintacki, a desert tycoon who has his own very special plans for the future of America. Then Hammett is kidnapped by Pintacki's torpedoes and Peters must act alone – and fast.
192pp / Crime Fiction / £3.50pb / 'A' format / 0 948353 75 9 / May 1990(Early export edition), July 1990(home)

Arthur Lyons
ALL GOD'S CHILDREN
Jacob Asch's first ever case leads him on a search for attractive 18 year old runaway to the L.A. fringe life of Jesus freaks and vicious motor bike gangs.
'A thoroughly professional job ... Lyons writes lean prose' – **N.Y. Times Book Review**
224pp/Crime Fiction/£3.50pb/'A' format/0 948353 66 X/January 1990

Pele, with Herb Resnicow
THE WORLD CUP MURDER
A marvellously entertaining thriller set around the World Cup Final with a mix of football lore, big business and murder as the deeply unpopular manager of the World Cup Finalists, America(!!), Yugoslav entrepreneur, Gregor Ragusic is murdered on the eve of the final. Pele brings his years of knowledge and skill to a story line deftly crafted by Herb Resnicow that adds up to a Dick Francis of football thrillers.
320pp/Crime Fiction/£3.99pb/'A' format/0 948353 74 0/May 1990

Dorothy B Hughes
IN A LONELY PLACE
Accepted as one of the best portraits ever of a psychopathic serial killer.
Dix Steele, recently demobbed lives in someone else's apartment in L.A. and uses their possessions and periodically follows women round the city. Dix looks up his old war buddy, now L.A. detective, Brub Nicolai. Dix feels an unreasonable resentment to Nicolai's lovely wife, Sylvia, but continues to see him often in the company of would be actress, Laurel, who he is fiercely possessive of.
When Laurel betrays Dix, the serial killings that Nicolai has been investigating and keeping his friend Dix informed of, step up in pace!
In a Lonely Place was filmed by Nicholas Ray in 1950, starring Humphrey Bogart.
192pp/Crime Fiction/£3.99pb/'A' format/0 948353 67 8

STILL TO COME:

Mirror, Mirror on the Wall – Stanley Ellin

Child Proof – Michael Lewin

Murder among Children – Tucker Coe

At the Hands of Another – Arthur Lyons

NO EXIT PRESS

BOOK
TOKEN

NO EXIT PRESS

NO EXIT PRESS Tokens allow the regular reader of NO EXIT PRESS titles to benefit. Each token at the end of the book is worth 50p. Just tear out the page, complete the order form, listing the titles you require and send it DIRECT to Oldcastle Books, 18 Coleswood Road, Harpenden, Herts AL5 1EQ. Please note this offer is ONLY available DIRECT from the publishers.

There is no limit to the number of tokens you can use against each book. For example if you have 6 tokens (value £3) you can send for a £2.99 book – and it won't cost you a penny – not even the postage! Alternatively you can use just one token and the price would be £2.99 less £0.50 = £2.49+£0.25 (10% p&p) = Total cost of £2.74.

Please note only the original page from the book is acceptable – no photocopies allowed.

ORDER FORM

1) .... £

2) .... £

3) .... £

4) .... £

Book Total .... £

Add 10% p&p contribution .... £

Total .... £

Less ... Tokens @ £0.50 each .... £

NET TOTAL ENCLOSED .... £

Please make cheques, P.O.s payable to Oldcastle Books Ltd or quote your credit card no. and expiry date.

VISA/ACCESS Expiry Date ☐ ☐ ☐ ☐

Card No. ☐ ☐ ☐ ☐ ☐ ☐ ☐ ☐ ☐ ☐ ☐ ☐ ☐ ☐ ☐

Signature ....

Name ....

Address ....

.... Postcode ....

Title of Book from which token comes from:

Name of Bookshop where Book bought: